Rose Wilder Lane
Her Story

Rose Wilder Lane contains new material added to the original version of this part of her life published by Rose herself in 1919 as *Diverging Roads*.

Rose Wilder Lane

Her Story

Rose Wilder Lane
and
Roger Lea MacBride

𝕊𝔹

A SCARBOROUGH BOOK
Stein and Day/Publishers/Scarborough House

SECOND SCARBOROUGH BOOKS PRINTING **1982**
Rose Wilder Lane: Her Story was originally published in
hardcover by Stein and Day/ *Publishers* in 1977
Copyright © 1977 by Wildrose Productions
All rights reserved
Printed in the United States of America

STEIN AND DAY/ *Publishers*
Scarborough House
Briarcliff Manor, N.Y. 10510

Library of Congress Cataloging in Publication Data

Lane, Rose Wilder, 1886-1968.
Rose Wilder Lane: her story.

1. Lane, Rose Wilder, 1886-1968 — Biography — Youth.
  2. Authors, American — 20th century — Biography.
  I. MacBride, Roger Lea, 1929-   joint author.
PS3523.A553Z524 1977   813'.5'2[B]   77-12072
ISBN 0-8128-6077-2 (pbk.)

This one is for Carol and Don Lemons,
with deep affection

I want to acknowledge the great help given me in this project by my partner and friend, Edwin Friendly, Jr. He read the manuscript in its several revisions and made numerous suggestions for improvement, most of which were invaluable.

Introduction

Rose Wilder Lane was a great person.

In the early days she had the great good fortune of being raised by Laura Ingalls Wilder and Almanzo Wilder. *They* had grown up as American pioneers. According to Laura: "I had seen the whole frontier, the woods, the Indian country of the great plains, the frontier towns, the building of railroads in wild, unsettled country, homesteading and farmers coming in to take possession. I realized that I had seen and lived it all—all the successive phases of the frontier, first the frontiersman, then the pioneer, then the farmers, and the towns. Then I understood that in my own life I represented a whole period of American history." And later she wrote about it in her famous "Little House" books.

With such a parent it was natural for Rose to grow up with wider horizons than most children in the last decade of the 19th century. And with such a background it was natural for Rose to become a pioneer herself in other areas. But especially a pioneer in building a singularly independent life for a woman of her time.

This book covers the first part of that building process: Rose Wilder left her secure Missouri home to make a new and very modern life for herself in California. True, not all of the places or the chronology of events are precisely as history would record them. They nonetheless accurately reflect the incredible life Rose Wilder Lane lived. She was a woman who made a way for herself in a world that had not yet accepted a woman's right to do what she wanted to do and be what she wanted to be; her right to live her life as she saw fit, to express herself through her talents and to deal with all issues, including those of morals, on her own terms.

Rose knew that in telling a true story precision of detail matters not. Truth, when the word is applied to a Rose, far transcends ordinary ties to reality. It is with that sure knowledge that a grandson offers to you her perfectly genuine fictional autobiography.

Charlottesville, Va.   Roger Lea MacBride
May, 1977

Part I

Chapter 1

There is a peculiar quality in the somnolence of a town in which little has occurred for many years. It is the unease of relaxation without repose, the unease of one who lies too late in bed, aware he should be getting up. Energy struggles feebly under the weight of the slow, uneventful days, but its pressure is always there, an urge that becomes an irritation in young blood.

Rose Wilder, pausing in the doorway of the post office on a warm spring afternoon, said to herself that she would be glad never to see Mansfield again. The familiar sight of its one drowsy street, the rickety wooden awnings over the sidewalks, the boys pitching horseshoes in the shade of the blacksmith shop, was almost insupportable.

She did not want to stand there looking at it. She did not want to follow the old stale road home to the old farmhouse, which had not changed since she could remember. She felt that she should be doing something, she did not know what.

A long purple curl of smoke unrolling over the bronze mist of bare apple orchards on Patterson's Hill was the plume of Number Five coming in. Men sauntered past, going toward the railroad station. The postmaster appeared in his shirt-sleeves, pushing a wheelbarrow filled with mail sacks down the middle of the street. The afternoon hack from Springfield rattled by, bringing a couple of tired, dust-grimed drummers. And the Mansfield girls, bare-headed, laughing, talking in high, gay voices came hurrying from the post-office, from the drugstore, from one of their Embroidery Club meetings, to see Number Five come in. Rose shifted the weight of the package on her arm, pulled her sunbonnet farther over her face, and started home.

An unaccustomed revolt struggled in her mind. She passed the wide, empty doorway of the livery stable, the glowing forge of the blacksmith-shop, without seeing them, absorbed in the turmoil of her thoughts. But at the corner where the gravel walk began, and the street became a country road slipping down a little slope between scattered white cottages, her self-absorption vanished.

A boy was walking slowly down the path. The elaborate unconcern of his attitude, the stiffness of his self-conscious back, told her that he had been waiting for her, and a rush of dizzying emotion swept away all but the immediate moment. The sunshine was warm on her shoulders, the grass of the lawns was green, every lace-curtained window behind the rose-bushes seemed to conceal watching eyes, and the sound of her feet on the gravel was loud in her ears. She overtook him at last, trying not to walk too fast. They smiled at each other.

"Hello, Paul," she said shyly.

He was a muscular, dark-haired boy with blue eyes. The young girl and boy were in the same class, the class that would graduate that spring. He was studying hard, trying to get as much education as possible before he would have to go to work. His father, a railroad engineer, had been killed in a wreck five years before, and Paul lived with his mother in a little house near the edge of town on the road to the farm.

"Hello," he replied. He cleared his throat. "I—had to go to the post-office to mail a letter," he said.

"Did you?" she answered. She tried to think of something else to say. "Will you be glad when school's over?" she asked.

Paul and she stood at the head of the class. He was better in arithmetic, but she beat him in spelling. For a long time they had exchanged glances of mutual respect across the schoolroom. Someone had told her that Paul said she was all right. He had beat her in arithmetic that day. "She takes a licking as well as a boy," was what he had said. But she had gone home and looked in the mirror.

The flutter at her heart had stopped then. No, she was not pretty. Her features were too large, her forehead too high. She despised the face that looked back at her. She longed for tiny, pretty features, large brown eyes, a low forehead with curling hair. The eyes in the mirror were gray and the hair was straight and brown. Not even a pretty, light brown. It was almost black. For the first time she had desperately wanted to be pretty. But now meeting him on the country road she did not care. He had waited for her, anyway.

They walked slowly under the arch of the trees, through the branches of which the sun sent long, slanting rays of light. There was a colored haze over the leafless orchards, and the hills were freshly green from the rains.

"Well, I've got a job promised as soon as school is over," said Paul.

"What kind of job?" she asked.

"Working at the depot. It pays fifteen a month to start," he replied. It was as if they were uttering poetry. The words did not matter. What they said did not matter.

"That's fine," she said. "I wish I had a job."

"Gee, I hate to see a girl go to work," said Paul.

His lips were full and very firm. When he set them

tightly, as he did then, he looked determined. There was something obstinate about the line of his chin and the slight frown between his heavy black brows. Her whole nature seemed to melt and flow toward him.

"I don't see why!" she flashed. "A girl like me has to work if she's going to get anywhere. I bet I could do as well as a boy if I had a chance."

The words were like a defensive armor between her and her real desire. She did not want to work. She wanted to be soft and pretty, tempting and teasing and sweet. She wanted to win the things she desired by tears and smiles and coaxing. But she did not know how.

Paul looked at her admiringly. He said, "I guess you could, all right. You're pretty smart for a girl."

She glowed with pleasure.

They had often walked along this road as far as his house, when accident brought them home from school at the same time. But their talk had never had this indefinable quality, as vague and beautiful as the misty color over the orchards.

Sometimes she had stopped at his house for a few minutes. His mother was a little woman with brisk, bustling manner. She always stood at the door to see that they wiped their feet before they went in. The house was very neat. There was an ingrain carpet on the front-room floor, swept till every thread showed. The center-table had a crocheted tidy on it and a Bible and a polished sea-shell. This room rose like a picture in her mind as they neared the gate. She did not want to leave Paul, but she did not want to go into that room with him now.

"Look—wait a minute—" he said, stopping in the gateway. "I wanted to tell you—" He turned red and looked down at one toe, boring into the soft ground. "About this being valedictorian—"

There had been a fierce rivalry between them for the

honor of being valedictorian at the graduating exercises. There was nothing to choose between them in scholarship, but Paul had won. She knew the teachers had decided she did not dress well enough to take such a prominent part. Or was it also because she was a girl?

"I hope you don't feel bad, Rose," he went on awkwardly. "I told them I'd give it up, because you're a girl, and anyway you ought to have it, I guess. I don't feel right about taking it, some way."

"That's all right," she answered. "I don't care about it."

She could see that he was very much relieved. She was glad she had lied. "Come in and look at what I've got in the shed," he said, getting away from the subject as quickly as possible.

She followed him around the house. He had cleared out the woodshed and put in a table and a chair. On the table stood a telegraphic-sounder and key, and a round, red, dry battery.

"I'm going to learn to be an operator," he said. "I've got most of the alphabet already. Listen." He made the instrument click. "I'm going to practice receiving, listening to the wires in the depot. Morrison says I can after I get through work. Telegraph-operators make as much as seventy dollars a month, and some of them, on the fast wires, make a hundred. I guess the train-dispatcher makes more than that."

"Oh, Paul, really?" She was all enthusiasm. He let her try the key. "I could do it. I know I could," she said.

He was encouraging.

"Sure you could." But there was a faint condescension in his tone, and she felt that he was entering a life into which she could not follow him.

"That's the trouble—*you* can get out and do things like that. A girl hasn't any chance at all."

"Oh, yes, she has," he answered. "There's lots of girl

operators. There's one down the line. Her father's station agent. And up at Rollo there's a man and his wife that handle the station between them. He works nights, and she works daytimes. They live over the depot, and if anything goes wrong she can call him."

"That must be nice," she said.

"He's pretty lucky, all right," Paul agreed. "It isn't exactly like having her working, of course—right together like that. I guess maybe they couldn't have been married unless she did work. He didn't have much, I guess. You know, he isn't so awfully much older than—but anyway, I'd hate to see—anybody I cared about going to work," he finished desperately. He opened and shut the telegraph-key, and the metallic clacks of the sounder were loud in the stillness. Unsaid things hung between them.

The palpitant moment was ended by the sound of his mother's voice. "Paul! Paul, I want some wood." They laughed shakily.

"I—I guess I better be going," she said. He made no protest. But when they stood in the woodshed doorway he said all in a rush:

"Look here. If I get a buggy next Sunday, what do you say we go driving somewhere?"

She carried those words home with her, singing as she went.

Chapter 2

Rose had been ready, waiting, long before she saw the buggy coming down the road that Sunday afternoon.

She had tried to do her hair in a new way, putting it up in rag curlers the night before, working with it for hours that morning in the stuffy attic bedroom before the wavy mirror, combing it, putting it up, taking it down again, with a nervous fluttering in her wrists. In the end she gave it up. She rolled the long braid into its usual mass at the nape of her neck, and pinned on it a black ribbon bow.

She longed for a new white dress to wear that day. Her pink gingham, whose blue-and-white plaid pattern had faded to blurred lines of mauve and pale pink, was hideous to her as she contemplated it stretched in all its freshly ironed stiffness on the bed. But it was the best she could do.

While she dressed, the sounds of the warm, lazy, spring morning floated in to her through the half-open window. The whinnying of the long-legged colt in the barnyard, the troubled, answering neigh of his mother from the pasture, the cackling of the hens, blended like the notes of a pastoral orchestra. The murmur of her father's talk with a neighbor in the side-yard came up to her; she heard without listening, and the sounds ran like an undercurrent of contentment in her thoughts.

When she had pinned her collar and put on her straw sailor-hat she stood for a long time gazing into the eyes that looked back at her from the mirror, lost in a formless reverie.

"Rose!" Laura said when she appeared in the kitchen. "What're you all dressed up for, this time of day?"

"I'm going driving," she answered, constrained. Her mother stopped, the oven door half open, a fork poised in her hand.

"Who with?"

"Paul." She tried to say the name casually, making an effort to meet her mother's eyes as usual.

Laura paused, then turned back to the stove. Well, she said, even if Rose were going out with a beau, that was no reason she shouldn't eat something. Dinner wouldn't be ready till two o'clock, but she ought to drink some milk anyway. Rose answered that she was not hungry.

Paul would come by one o'clock, she thought. His mother had only a cold lunch on Sundays, because they went to church. He came ten minutes late, and she had forgotten everything else in the strain of waiting.

She met him at the gate, and he got out to help her into the buggy-seat. He was wearing his Sunday clothes, the blue suit, carefully brushed and pressed, and a stiff white collar. He looked strange and formal.

"It isn't much of a rig," he said apologetically, clearing his throat. She recognized the bony sorrel and the rattling buggy, the cheapest in Mansfield's only livery stable. But even that, she knew, was an extravagance for Paul.

"It's hard to get a rig on Sunday," she said. "Everybody takes them all out in the morning. I think you were very lucky to get such a good one. Isn't it a lovely day?"

"It looks like the rains are about over," he replied in a polite voice. After the first radiant glance they had not looked at each other. He chirped to the sorrel, and they drove away together.

Enveloped in the hood of the buggy-top, they saw before them the yellow road, winding on among the trees, disappearing, appearing again like a ribbon looped about the curves of the hills. There was gold in the green of the fields, gold in the poppies beside the road, gold in the ruddiness of young apricot twigs. The clear air itself was filled with vibrant, golden sunshine. They drove in a golden haze. What did they say? It did not matter. They looked at each other.

His arm lay along the back of the buggy seat. Its being there was like a secret shared between them, a knowledge held in common, to be cherished and to be kept unspoken. When the increasing consciousness of it grew too poignant to be borne any longer in silence they escaped from it in sudden mutual panic, breathless. They left the buggy, tying the patient sorrel in the shade beneath a tree, and clambered up the hillside.

They went, they said, to gather wild flowers. He took her hand to help her up the trail, and she permitted it, stumbling, when unaided she could have climbed more easily, glad to feel that he was the leader, eager that he should think himself the stronger. At the top of the hill they came to a low-spreading live-oak with a patch of young grass beneath it, and here, forgetting the ungathered flowers, they sat down.

They sat there a long time, talking very seriously on grave subjects; life and the meaning of it, the bigness of the universe, and how it makes a fellow feel funny, somehow, when he looks at the stars at night and thinks about things. She understood. She felt that way herself sometimes. It was amazing to learn how many things they had felt in common. Neither of them had ever expected to find any one else who felt them, too.

Then there was the question of what to do with your life. It was a pretty important thing to decide. You didn't want to make mistakes, like so many men did. You had to start right. That was the point, the start. When you get to be eighteen or so, almost twenty, you realize that, and you look back over your life and see how you've wasted a lot of time already. You realize you'd better begin to do something.

Now here was the idea of learning telegraphy. That looked pretty good. If a fellow really went at that and worked hard, there was no telling what it might lead to. You might get to be a train-dispatcher or even a railroad superintendent. There were lots of big men who didn't have any better start than he had. Look at Edison.

She agreed. She was sure there was nothing he could not do. Somehow, then, they began to talk as if she would be with him. She might be a telegrapher, too. Wouldn't it be fun if she was, so they could be in the same town? He'd help her with the train orders, and if he worked nights she could fix his lunch for him.

They made a sort of play of it, laughing about it. They were only supposing, of course. They carefully refrained from voicing the thought that clamored behind everything they said, that set her heart racing and kept her eyes from meeting his, the thought of that young couple at Rollo.

And at the last, when they could no longer ignore the incredible fact that the afternoon was gone, that only a golden western sky behind the flat, blue mass of the hills remained to tell of the vanished sunlight, they rose reluctantly, hesitant. He had taken her two hands to help her to her feet. In the grayness of the twilight they looked at each other, and she felt the approach of a moment tremendous, irrevocable.

He was drawing her closer. She felt, with the pull of his hands, an urging within herself, a compulsion like a strong current, sweeping her away, merging her with something unknown, vast, beautifully terrible. Suddenly, in a panic, pushing him blindly away, she heard herself saying, "No! Please—" The tension of his arms relaxed.

"All right—if you don't want—I didn't mean—" he stammered. Their hands clung for a moment, uncertainly, then dropped apart. They stumbled down the dusky trail and drove home almost in silence.

Spring came capriciously that year. It smiled unexpectedly upon the hills through long days of golden sunshine, coaxing wild flowers from the damp earth and swelling buds with her warm promise. It retreated again behind cold skies, abandoning eager petals and sap-filled twigs to the chill desolation of rain and the bitterness of frost.

Farmers trudging behind their plows felt it coming in the stir of the scented air, in the responsiveness of the springy soil and, looking up at the sparkling skies, felt a warmth in their own veins even while they shook their heads doubtfully. And rising in the dawns they tramped the orchard rows, bending tips of branches between anxious fingers, pausing to cut open a few buds on their calloused palms.

To Rose the days were like notes in a melody. Linnets' songs and sunshine streaming through the attic windows or gray panes and rain on the roof were one to her. She woke to either as to a holiday. She slipped from beneath the patchwork quilt into a cold room and dressed with shivering fingers; life was too good to be wasted in sleep. She seemed made of energy as she ran down the steep stairs to the kitchen. It swelled in her veins as a river frets against its banks in the spring floods.

Every sight and sound struck upon her senses with a new freshness. There was exhilaration in the bite of cold water on her skin when she washed in the tin basin on the bench by the door, and the smell of coffee and frying salt pork was good. She sang while she spread the red table-cloth on the kitchen table and set out the plates.

She sang:

You're as welcome as the flowers in Ma-a-ay,
And I love you in the same o-o-old way.

It seemed to her that she was caroling aloud poetry so exquisite that all its meaning escaped the ears about her. She walked among them, alone, wrapped in a glory no one else could perceive.

Even her mother's tight-lipped anxiety did not quite break through her happy absorption. Laura worked silently, stepping heavily about the kitchen, now and then glancing through the window toward the barn. When Almanzo came clumping up the path and stopped at the back steps to scrape the mud from his boots, she went to the door and opened it, saying almost harshly, "Well?"

Rose's father said nothing, continuing for a moment to knock a boot heel against the edge of the step. Then he came slowly in, and began to dip water from the water pail into the wash-basin. The slump of his body in the sweat-stained overalls expressed nothing but weariness.

"I guess last night settled it," he said. "We won't get enough of a crop to pay to pick it. Out of twenty buds I cut on the south slope only four weren't black."

Laura went back to the stove and turned the salt pork, holding her head back from the spatters. "What are we going to do about the mortgage?" The question filled a long silence. Rose's song was hushed, though the echoes of it still went on in some secret place within her, safe there even from this calamity.

"Same as we've always done, I guess," her father answered at last, lifting a dripping face and reaching for the roller towel. "See if I can get young Craig to renew it."

"Well, he will. Surely he will," Rose said. Her tone of cheerfulness was like a slender shaft splintering against a stone wall. "And there must be *some* fruit left. If there isn't much of a crop what we do get ought to bring pretty good prices, too."

"You're right it ought to," Almanzo replied bitterly. "A good crop never brings 'em."

"Well, anyway, I'm through school now, and I'll be doing something," Rose said. She had no clear idea what it would be, but suddenly she felt in her youth and happiness a strength that her discouraged father and mother did not have, and she felt that she could take them up in her arms and carry them triumphantly to comfort and peace.

"Eat your breakfast and don't talk nonsense," her father said.

But her victorious mood revived while she washed the dishes. She felt older, stronger, and more confident than she had ever been. The news of the killing frost was to Rose a call to action.

That afternoon when the ironing was finished she dressed in her pink gingham and best shoes. She was going to town for the mail, she explained to her mother, and when Laura said, "Why, you went day before yesterday!" she replied, "Well, I guess I'll just go to town, anyway. I feel like walking somewhere."

Her mother apparently accepted the explanation without further thought. The blindness of other people astonished Rose. It seemed to her that every blade of grass in the fields, every scrap of white cloud in the sky, knew that she was going to see Paul.

She let her hand rest a moment on the gate as she went through. It was the gate on which they leaned when he brought her home from church on Sunday nights. She could feel his presence there still; she could almost see the dark mass of his shoulders against the starry sky, and the white blur of his face.

The long lane by the meadow was crowded with memories of him. Here they had stopped to gather poppies; there, just beside the gray stone, he had knelt one day to tie her shoe. On the little bridge shaded by the oak-trees they always stopped to lean on the rail and watch their reflections shot across by ripples of light in the stream below. She was dazzled by the beauty of the world as she went by all these places. It seemed to her that she had been blind all her life.

She stood some time on the little bridge, looking at all this loveliness, and she said his name to herself, under her breath "Paul." A quiver ran along her nerves at the sound of it.

He would be busy handling baggage at the railroad station when Number Five came in. She thought of his sturdy shoulders in the blue work-shirt, the smooth forehead under his ragged cap, the straight-looking blue eyes and firm lips. She would stand a little apart, by the window where the telegraph-keys were clicking, and he would pass, pushing a hand-truck through the crowd on the platform. Their eyes would meet, and the look would be like a bond subtly uniting them in an intimacy unperceived by the people who jostled them. Then she would go away, walking slowly through the town, and he would overtake her on his way home to supper. Her thoughts went no further than that. They stopped with Paul.

But before she reached his house she saw Sammy Harner frolicking in the road, hilarious in the first spring freedom of going barefoot. He skipped from side to side, his wide straw hat flapping; he shied a stone at a bird; he whistled shrilly between his teeth. When he saw her he sobered quickly and came trotting down the road, reaching her, panting.

"I was coming out to your house just's fast as I could," he said. "I got a note for you." He sought anxiously in his pockets, found it in the crown of his hat. "He gave me a nickle, and said to wait if they's an answer."

Excited, she tore open the railway company's yellow envelope and read:

Dear Friend Rose:

>I have got a new job and I have to go to California tonight where I am going to work. I would like to see you before I go, as I do not know when I can come back, but probably not for a long time. I did not know I was going till this afternoon and I have to go on the Cannonball. Can you meet me about eight o'clock by the bridge? I have to pack yet and I am afraid I cannot get time to come out to your house and I want to see you very much. Please answer by Sammy.

>Your friend, Paul

The familiar surroundings were suddenly unreal. "Tell him I didn't have a pencil," she said. "Tell him I said, 'Yes.'" And as Sammy lingered, watching her with unashamed curiosity, she added sharply, "Hurry! Hurry up now!"

It was a relief to sit down, when at last Sammy had disappeared around the bend in the road. The whirling world seemed to settle somewhat into place then. She had never thought of Paul's going away. She wondered dully if it were a good job, and if he were glad to go.

Chapter 3

She came down the road again a little after seven o'clock. The road lost itself in darkness before her, and the fields stretched out into a darkness that seemed illimitable, as endless as the sky. She felt herself part of the night.

For an eternity she walked up and down the road, stumbling in the ruts, waiting. Once she went as far as the top of the hill beyond the bridge, and saw shining against the blackness the yellow lights of his house. She looked at them for a long time. At last she saw him coming, and she stood still in the pool of darkness under the oaks until he reached her.

"Rose?" he said uncertainly. "Is it you?"

"Yes," she answered. Her throat ached.

"I came as quick as I could," he said. Somehow she knew that his throat ached, too. They moved to the little railing of the bridge and stood trying to see each other's faces in the gloom. "Are you cold?" he asked.

"No," she said. She saw then that the shawl had slipped from her shoulders and was dragging over one arm. The wind fluttered it, and her hands were clumsy, trying to pull it back into place.

"Here," he was taking off his coat. "No," she said again. But she let him wrap half the coat around her. They stood close together in the folds of it. The chilly wind flowed around them like water, and the warmth of their trembling bodies made a little island of cosiness in a sea of cold.

"I got to go," he said. "It's a good job. Fifty dollars a month. I got to support mother, you know. Her money's pretty nearly gone already, and she spent a lot putting me through school. I just got to go. I wish—I wish I didn't have to."

She tried to hold her lips steady.

"It's all right," she said. "I'm glad you got a good job."

"You mean you aren't going to miss me when I'm gone?"

"Yes, I'll miss you."

"I'm going to miss you an awful lot," he said huskily. "You going to write to me?"

"Yes, I'll write if you will."

"You aren't going to forget me—you aren't going to get to going with anybody else—are you?"

She could not answer. The trembling that shook them carried them beyond speech. Wind and darkness melted together in a rushing flood around them. The ache in her throat dissolved into tears, and they clung together, cheek against hot cheek, in voiceless misery.

"Oh, Rose! Oh, Rose!" She was crushed against the beating of his heart, his arms hurt her. She wanted them to hurt her. "You're so—you're so—sweet!" he stammered, and gropingly they found each other's lips.

Words came back to her after a time.

"I don't want you to go away," she sobbed.

His arms tightened around her, then slowly relaxed. His chin lifted, and she knew that his mouth was setting into its firm lines again.

"I got to," he said. The finality of the words was like something solid beneath their feet once more.

"Of course; I didn't mean—" She moved a little away from him, smoothing her hair with a shaking hand.

"I got to think about things," he said.

"Yes—I know."

"There's mother. Fifty dollars a month. We just can't—"

Tears were welling slowly from her eyes and running down her cheeks. She was not able to stop them.

"No," she said. "I've got to do something to help at home, too." She groped for the shawl at her feet. He picked it up and wrapped it carefully around her. A new solemnity had descended upon them both. They felt dimly that life had changed for them, that it would never be the same again.

They walked up and down in the starlight, trying to talk soberly, feeling very old and sad, a weight on their hearts. He was going to be night operator at the station in a town named Ripley, in the San Joaquin valley, he told her. He could not keep a shade of self-importance from his voice, but he explained conscientiously that there would not be much telegraphing. Very few train orders were sent there at night. But it was a good job for a beginner and pretty soon maybe he would be able to get a better one. Say, when he was twenty or twenty-one, seventy-five dollars a month perhaps. It wouldn't be long to wait.

They were clinging together again. Their kisses were salty with tears.

He left Rose at her gate. The memory of all the times they had stood there was the last unbearable pain. They held each other tight, without speaking.

"You—haven't said—tell me you—love me," he said after a long time.

"I love you," she said, as though it were a sacrament. He was silent for another moment, and in the dim starlight she felt rather than saw a strange, half-terrifying expression on his face.

"Will you go away with me—right now—and marry me— if I ask you to?" His voice was hoarse.

She felt that she was taking all she was or could be in her cupped hands and offering it to him.

"Yes," she said.

His whole body shook with a long sob. "If—if only we could!" He tried to say more, choking, tearing himself roughly away from her. She saw him going down the road, almost running, and then the darkness hid him.

In the days that followed it seemed to Rose that she could have borne the separation better if she had not been left behind. He had gone down the shining lines of track beyond Patterson's Hill into a vague big world that baffled her thoughts. He wrote that he had been in San Francisco and taken a ride on a sight-seeing car. It was a splendid place, he said; he wished she could see the things he saw. He had seen Chinatown, the Presidio, the beach, and Seal Rocks. Then he had gone on to Ripley, which wasn't much like Mansfield. He was well, and hoped she was, and he thought of her every day and was hers lovingly. But she felt that she was losing touch with him, and when she contemplated two or three years of waiting she felt that she would lose him entirely. She thought again of that young couple at Rollo, and pangs of envy were added to the misery in which she was living.

He had been gone two weeks when she announced to her mother that she was going to be a telegraph-operator. She held to the determination with a tenacity that surprised even herself. She argued, she pleaded, she pointed out the wages she would earn, the money she could send home. There was a notice in the Mansfield weekly paper, advertising a school of telegraphy in Sacramento, saying: "Operators in great demand. Graduates earn $75 to $100 a month up." She wrote to that school, and immediately a reply came, assuring her that she could learn in three months, that railroad and telegraph companies were clamoring for operators, that the school guaranteed all its graduates good positions. The tuition was fifty dollars.

Her father said he guessed that settled it.

But in the end she won. When Almanzo renewed the mortgage for another year he borrowed an extra hundred dollars from the bank for tuition and expenses. Fifty dollars seemed a fortune on which to live for three months. Laura and Rose went over her clothes together, and Laura gave her the telescope-bag in which to pack them.

A new intimacy grew up between the two while they worked. Her mother said it was just as well for her to have a good job for a while. Maybe she wouldn't make a bad mistake getting married before she was sure she knew her own mind.

"But I want you to promise me if anything comes up that looks as if it isn't just right, you let me know right away," Laura said. "I'm going to be worried about you, off alone in a city like that."

She promised quickly, uncertainly, and her mother began to talk of something else. Mrs. Updike, who lived on the next farm, was going out to San Francisco to visit her sister. She would go with Rose to Sacramento and see her settled there. Rose must be sure to eat her meals regularly and keep her clothes mended and write every week and study hard. She promised all those things.

There was a flurry on the last morning. Laura unpacked the bag a dozen times to be sure that nothing was left out. Rose and her parents drove to town, crowded into the two-seated light wagon, and there was another flurry at the station when the train came in. She hugged Laura and Almanzo awkwardly, smiling with tears in her eyes. She felt, not for the first time, how much she loved them.

Until the train rounded the curve west of town Rose gazed back at Mansfield and the little yellow station where Paul had worked. Then she settled back against red velvet cushions to watch unfamiliar trees and hills flashing backward past the windows. She had an excited sense of adventure, wondering what the school would be like, promising herself again to study hard.

During the days of travel, through the changing of trains and transfers of baggage, Rose and Mrs. Updike worried at intervals, fearing that by some mischance Mr. Weeks, the manager of the school, would fail to meet them at the Sacramento station. They wore bits of red yarn in their buttonholes so that he would recognize them.

He was waiting when the train stopped. He was a young, thin, well-dressed man, with a face that seemed oddly old, like a half-ripe apple withered. He hurried them through noisy, bustling streets, on and off streetcars, up a stairway at last to the school.

There were two rooms, a small one, which was the office, and a larger one, bare and not very clean, lighted by two high windows looking out on an alley. In the large room were half a dozen tables, each with a telegraph-sounder and key upon it. There was no one there at the moment, Mr. Weeks explained, because it was Saturday afternoon. The school usually did no business on Saturday afternoons, but he would make an exception for Rose. If she liked, he said briskly, she could pay him the tuition now, and begin her studies early Monday morning. He was sure she would be a good operator, and he guaranteed her a good position when she graduated. He would even give her a written guarantee, if she wished. But she did not ask for that. It would have seemed to imply a doubt of Mr. Weeks' good faith.

Mrs. Updike, panting from climbing the stairs and nervous with anxiety about catching her return train to San Francisco, asked him about rooms. Providentially, he knew a very good one and cheap, next door to the school. He was kind enough to take them to see it.

There were a number of rooms in a row, all opening on a long hallway reached by stairs from the street. They were kept by Mrs. Brown, who managed the restaurant downstairs. She was a sallow little woman, with very bright brown eyes and yellow hair. She talked continuously in a light, mechanically gay voice, making quick movements with her hands and moving about the room with a whisking of silk petticoats, driven, it seemed, by an intensity of energy almost feverish.

The room rented for six dollars a month. It had a large bow-window overlooking the street, gaily flowered wall-paper, a red carpet, a big wooden bed, a wash-stand with pitcher and bowl, and two rocking chairs. At the end of the long hall was a bathroom with a white tub in it, the first Rose had seen. There was something metropolitan about that tub; a bath in it would be an event far different from the Saturday night scrubs in the tin wash-tub at home. And she could eat in the restaurant below; very good meals for twenty cents, or even for less if she wanted to buy a meal-ticket.

"I guess it's as good as you can do," said Mrs. Updike.

"I think it's lovely," Rose said.

So it was settled. Rose gave Mrs. Brown six dollars, and she whisked away after saying: "I'm sure you'll like it, dearie, and if there's anything you want, let me know. I sleep right in the next room, so nothing's going to bother you, and if you get lonesome, just come and knock on my door."

Then Mrs. Updike, with a hasty farewell peck at her cheek, hurried away to catch her train. Mr. Weeks went with her to the station, and Rose was left alone.

She locked her door first, and counted her money, feeling very businesslike. Then she unpacked her bag and put away her things, pausing now and then to look around the room that was hers. It seemed very large and luxurious. She felt a pleasant sense of responsibility when everything was neatly in order and she stood at the window, looking down the street to the corner where at intervals she saw streetcars passing. She promised herself to work very hard, and to pay back soon the money her father had lent her, with interest.

Then she thought, smiling, that in a little while she would go downstairs and eat supper in a restaurant, and then she would buy a tablet and pencil and, coming back to this beautiful room, she would sit down all alone and write a letter to Paul.

Chapter 4

The thought of Paul was the one clear reality in Rose's life while she blundered through the first months in Sacramento. It was the only thing that warmed her in the midst of the strangeness that surrounded her.

There was the school. She did not know what she had expected, but she felt vaguely that she had not found it. Faithfully every morning at eight o'clock she was at her table in the dingy back room, struggling to translate the dots and dashes of the Morse alphabet into crisp, even clicks of the sounder. There were three other pupils, farm boys who moved their necks uncomfortably in stiff collars and reddened when they looked at her.

There was a wire from that room into the front office. Sometimes its sounder opened, and they knew that Mr. Weeks was going to send them something to copy. They moved to that table eagerly. There were days when the sounder did not click again, and after a while one of the boys would tiptoe to the office and report that Mr. Weeks was asleep. On other days the sounder would tap for a long time meaninglessly, while they looked at each other in bewilderment. Then it would make a few shaky letters and stop and make a few more.

Then for several days Mr. Weeks would not come to the

school at all. They sank into a kind of stupor, sitting in the close, warm room, while flies buzzed on the windowpane. Rose's moist finger tips stuck to the hard rubber of the key; it was an effort to remember the alphabet. But she kept at work doggedly, knowing how much depended upon her success. Always before her was the vision of the station where she would work with Paul, a little yellow station with housekeeping rooms upstairs. She thought, too, of the debt she owed her father, and the help she could give him later when she was earning money.

Bit by bit she learned a little about the other pupils. Two of them had come down from Mendocino County together. They had worked two summers to earn the money, and yet they had been able to save only seventy-five dollars for the tuition. However, they had been sharp enough to persuade Mr. Weeks to take them for that sum. They lived together in one room, and cooked their meals over the gas-jet.

One of the boys had a more knowing air than the other and smoked cigarettes as well. He swaggered a little, giving them to understand that he was a man of the world and knew all the wickedness of the city. He looked at Rose with eyes she did not like, and once asked her to go to a show with him. Although she was very lonely and had never seen a show in a real theater, she refused. She felt that Paul would not like her to go. At the end of three months in Sacramento these were the only people she knew, except Mrs. Brown.

She felt that she would like Mrs. Brown if she knew her better. Her shyness kept her from saying more than "Good evening," when she handed her meal-ticket over the restaurant counter to be punched, and for some inexplicable reason Mrs. Brown seemed shy with her. It was her own fault, Rose thought; Mrs. Brown laughed and talked gaily with the men customers, cajoling them into buying cigars and chewing-gum from her little stock.

Rose speculated about Mr. Brown. She never saw him; she felt quite definitely that he was not alive. Yet Mrs. Brown often looked at her wide wedding-ring, turning it on her finger as if she were not quite accustomed to wearing it. A widow, and so young! Rose's heart ached at the thought of that brief romance. Mrs. Brown's thin figure and bright yellow hair were those of a girl; only her eyes were old. It must be grief that had given them that hard, weary look. Rose smiled at her wistfully over the counter, longing to express her friendliness and sympathy. But Mrs. Brown's manner always baffled her.

These meetings were not frequent. Rose tried to make her three-dollar meal ticket last a month, and that meant that only five times a week she could sit in state, eating warm food in an atmosphere thick with smells of coffee and stew and hamburger steak. She had learned that cinnamon rolls could be bought for half price on Saturday nights, and she kept a bag of them in her room, and some fruit. This made her a little uneasy when she saw Mrs. Brown's anxious eye on the vacant tables; she felt that she was defrauding Mrs. Brown by eating in her room.

Mrs. Brown worked very hard, Rose knew. It was she who swept the hall and kept the rooms in order. She did not do it very well, but Rose saw her sometimes in the evenings working at it. She swept with quick, feverish strokes. Her yellow hair straggled over her face; her high heels clicked on the floor; her petticoats made a whisking sound. There was something piteous about her, as there is about a little trained animal on the stage, set to do tasks for which it is not fitted. Rose stole down the hallway at night, taking the broom from its corner as if she was committing a theft, and surreptitiously swept and dusted her own room, so that Mrs. Brown would not have to do it.

She wished that it took more time. When she had finished there was nothing to do but sit at her window and look down at the street. People went up and down, strolling leisurely in the warm summer evening. She saw girls in dainty dresses, walking about in groups, and the sight increased her loneliness. Buggies went by; a man with his wife and children out driving, a girl and her sweetheart. At the corner there was the clanging of street-cars, and she watched to see them passing, brightly lighted, filled with people. Once in a while she saw an automobile, and her breath quickened, she leaned from the window until it was out of sight. She felt then the charm of the city, with its crowds, its glitter, its strange, hurried life.

Two young men passed often down that street in an automobile. They looked up at her window when they went by and slowed the machine. If Rose were leaning on the sill, they waved to her and shouted gaily. She always pretended that she had not seen them and drew back, but she watched for the machine to pass again. It seemed to be a link between her and all the exciting life from which she was shut out. She would have liked to know those young men.

She sat at the window one evening near the end of the three months that she had planned to spend in the telegraph school. Paul's picture was in her hand. He had had it taken for her in Ripley. It was a beautiful shiny picture, cabinet size, showing him against a tropical background of palms and ferns.

He had taken off a derby, which he held somewhat self-consciously; his strong figure wore an air of prosperity in an unfamiliar suit.

She brooded upon the firm line of his chin, the clean-cut lips, the smooth forehead from which the hair was brushed back slickly. His neck was turned so that his eyes did not quite meet hers. It was baffling, that aloof gaze; it hurt a little. She wished that he would look at her. She felt that the picture would help her more if he would, and she needed help.

Mr. Weeks had returned from one of his long absences

that day, and she had taken courage to ask him about a job. He had listened while she stood beside his desk, stammering out her worry and her need. Her money was almost gone; she thought she telegraphed pretty well; she had studied hard. She watched his shaking hand fumbling with some papers on his desk, and felt pityingly that she should not bother him when he was sick. But desperation drove her on. She did not suspect the truth until he looked up at her with reddened eyes and answered incoherently. Then she saw that he was drunk.

Her shock of loathing came upon her in a wave of nausea. She trembled so that she could hardly get down the stairs, and she had walked a long time in the clean sunshine before the full realization of what it meant chilled her. She sat now confronting that realization.

She had only two dollars, a half-used meal-ticket and a week's rent paid in advance. She saw clearly that she could hope for nothing from the telegraph school. It did not occur to her to blame anybody. Her mind ran desperately from thought to thought, like a caged creature seeking escape between iron bars.

She could not go home. She could not live there again, defeated, knowing day by day that she had added a hundred dollars to the mortgage. She had told Paul so confidently that she could do as well as a boy if she had the chance, and she had had the chance. He could not help her. The street below was full of people going by, absorbed in their own concerns, careless of hers.

She had not seen the automobile with the two young men in it until it stopped across the street. Even then she looked at it with dull eyes. But the two young men were looking up at her window, talking together, looking up again. They were getting out. They crossed the street. She heard their voices below; a moment later her heart began to thump. They were coming up the stairs.

Something was going to happen. At last something was going to break the terrible loneliness and deadness. She stood listening, one hand at her throat, alert, breathless.

They were standing half-way up the stairs, talking. She felt indecision in the sound of their voices. One of them ran down again. There was an aching silence. Then she heard footsteps and the high, gay voice of Mrs. Brown. They were laughing together. "Oh, you Kittie!" one of the young men said. The three came up the stairs, and she heard their clattering steps and caught a word or two as they went past her room. Then the scratch of a match, and light gleamed through the crack of Mrs. Brown's door.

They went on talking. It appeared that they were arguing, coaxing, urging something. Mrs. Brown's voice put them off. There was a crash and laughter. She gathered that they were scuffling playfully. Later she heard Mrs. Brown's voice at the head of the back stairs, calling down to some one to send up some beer.

Her tenseness relaxed. She felt herself falling into bottomless depths of depression. The bantering argument was going on again. Meaningless scraps of it came to her while she undressed in the dark and crept into bed.

"Aw, come on Kittie, be a sport! A stunning looker like that! What're you after anyhow—money?"

"Cut that out. No, I tell you. What's it to you why I won't?"

Rose crushed her face into the pillow and wept silently. It seemed the last unkindness of fate that Mrs. Brown should give a party and not ask her.

Chapter 5

The next day Rose dressed very carefully in a fresh white waist and her Indianhead skirt and went down to the Western Union office to ask for a job. She knew where to find the office; she had often looked at its plate-glass front lettered in blue during her lonely walks on the crowded street. Her heart thumped loudly and her knees were weak when she went through the open door.

The big room was cut across by a long counter, on which a young man lounged in his shirt-sleeves, a green eyeshade pushed back on his head. Behind him telegraph instruments clattered loudly, disturbing the stifling quiet of the hot morning. The young man looked at her curiously.

"Manager? Won't I do?" he asked.

She heard her voice.

"I'd rather see him—if he's busy—I could wait."

The manager rose from the desk where he had been sitting. He was a tall, thin man, with thin hair combed carefully over the top of his head. His lips were thin, too, and there were deep creases on either side of his mouth, like parentheses.

"I'm sorry, I don't need another operator," he said, but his eyes looked her over, interested. "What experience do you have?"

She was a graduate of Weeks' School of Telegraphy, she

told him breathlessly. She could send perfectly; she wasn't so sure of her receiving, but she would be awfully careful not to make mistakes. She had to have a job, she just had to have a job; it didn't matter how much it paid, anything. She felt that she could not walk out of that office. She clung to the edge of the counter as if she were drowning and it were a life-line.

"Well, come in. I'll see what you can do," he said. He swung open a door in the counter, and Rose followed him between the tables. There was a dusty instrument on a battered desk, back by the big switchboard. The manager took a message from a hook and gave it to her. "Let's hear you send that."

Rose began painstakingly. The young man with the eyeshade had wandered over. He stood leaning against a table, listening, and after she had made a few letters she felt that a glance passed between him and the manager, over her head. She finished the message, even adding a careful period. She thought she had done very well. When she looked up the manager said kindly:

"Not so bad! You'll be an operator some day."

"If you'll only give me a chance," she pleaded.

He said that he would take her address and let her know. She felt that the young man was slightly amused. She gave the manager her name and the street number. He repeated it in surprise.

"You're staying with Kittie Brown?" Again a glance passed over her head. Both of them looked at her with intensified interest, for which she saw no reason. "Yes," she replied. She felt keenly that it was an awkward moment, and bewilderment added to her confusion. The young man turned away and, sitting down, began to send a pile of messages, working very busily, sending with his right hand and marking off the messages with his left. But she felt that his attention was still upon her and the manager.

"Well! And you want to work here?" The manager

rubbed one hand over his chin, smiling. "I don't know. I might."

"Oh, if you would!"

He hesitated for an agonizing moment.

"Well, I'll think about it. Come and see me again." He held her fingers warmly when they shook hands, and she returned the pressure gratefully. She felt that he was very kind. She felt, too, that she had conducted the interview very well, and returning hope warmed her while she went back to her room.

That afternoon she had a visitor. She had written her weekly letter to her mother, saying that she had almost finished school and was expecting to get a job, hesitating a long time, miserably, before she added that she did not have much money left and would like to borrow another five dollars. She had eaten a stale roll and an apple and was considering how long she could make the meal-ticket last when she heard the knock on her door.

She opened it in surprise, thinking there had been a mistake. A stout, determined-looking woman stood there, a well-dressed woman who wore black gloves and a veil. Immediately Rose felt herself young, inexperienced, a child in firm hands.

"You're Rose Wilder? I'm Mrs. Campbell." She stepped into the room, Rose giving way before her assured advance. She swept the place with one look. "What on earth was your mother thinking of, leaving you in a place like this? Did you know what you were getting into?"

"I don't know—what—won't you take a chair?" said Rose.

Mrs. Campbell sat down gingerly, very erect. They looked at each other.

"I might as well talk straight out to you," Mrs. Campbell said with a manner that suggested she said so often. "I met Mrs. Morris, Mrs. Updike's sister, at the Eastern Star convention in Oakland last week, and she told me about

you, and I promised to look you up. Well, when I found
out! I told Mr. Campbell I was coming straight down here
to talk to you. If you want to stay in a place like this, well
and good, it's your affair. Though I should feel it my duty
to write to your mother. I wouldn't want my own girl left
in a strange town, at your age, and nobody taking any
interest in her."

"I'm sure it's very kind." Rose murmured in
bewilderment.

"Well," Mrs. Campbell drew a long breath and plunged,
"I suppose you know the sort of person this Kittie Brown,
she calls herself, is? I suppose you know she's a bad
woman?"

A wave of blackness went through the girl's mind.

"Everybody in town knows what *she* is," Mrs. Campbell
continued. "*Everybody* knows that this place she runs is
nothing but a—" and she went on, her voice growing more
bitter. Rose half hearing the words, choked back a sick
impulse to ask her to stop talking. She felt that everything
about her was poisoned; she wanted to escape, to hide, to
feel that she would never be seen again by any one. When
the hard voice had stopped it was an effort to speak.

"But what will I do?"

"Do? I should think you'd want to get out of here just as
quick as you could."

"Oh, I do want to. But where can I go? My rent's paid. I
haven't any money."

Mrs. Campbell considered.

"Well, you will have money, won't you? Your folks don't
expect you to live here on nothing, do they? If it's only a
day or two, I could take you in myself rather than leave
you in a place like this. There's plenty of decent places in
town." She became practical. "The first thing to do's to
pack your things right away. How long is your rent paid?
Can't you get some of it back?"

She waited while Rose packed. She did not stop talking,

and Rose tried to answer her coherently and gratefully. She felt that she should be grateful. They went down the stairs, and Mrs. Campbell waited outside the restaurant while Rose went in to ask Mrs. Brown to refund the week's rent.

It was noon, but there were only one or two people in the restaurant. Mrs. Brown's smile faded when Rose stammered that she was leaving.

"You are? What's wrong? Anybody been bothering you?" Her glance fell upon the waiting Mrs. Campbell, and her sallow face whitened. "Oh, that's it, is it?"

"No," Rose said hastily. "That is, it's been very nice here, and I liked it, but a friend of mine—she wants me to stay with her. I'm sorry to leave, but I haven't much money." She struggled against feeling pity for Mrs. Brown. She choked over asking her to refund the rent.

Mrs. Brown said she could not do it. She offered, however, to give Rose something in trade, two dollars' worth. They both tried to make the transaction commonplace and dignified.

Rose, at a loss, pointed out a heap of peanut candy in the glass counter. She had often looked at it and wished she could afford to buy some. Mrs. Brown's thin hands shook, but she was piling the candy on the scale when Mrs. Campbell came in.

"What's she doing?" Mrs. Campbell asked Rose. "You buying candy?"

"I don't know what business it is of yours, coming interfering with me!" Mrs. Brown broke out. "I never did her any harm. I never even talked to her. You ask her if I ever bothered her. You ask her if I didn't leave her alone. You ask her if I ain't keeping a decent, respectable, quiet place and doing the best I can and minding my own business and trying to make a square living. You ask her what I ever did to her all the time she's been here." Her voice was high and shrill. Tears were rolling down her face.

Mechanically she went on breaking up the candy and piling it on the scales. "I don't know what I ever did to you that you don't leave me alone, coming poking around."

"I didn't come here to talk to you," said Mrs. Campbell. "Come on out of here," she commanded Rose.

"I wish to God you'd mind your own business!" Mrs. Brown cried after them. "If you'd only tend to your own affairs, you *good* people!" She hurled the words after them like a curse, her voice breaking with sobs. The door slammed under Mrs. Campbell's angry hand.

Rose, shaking and quivering, tried not to be sorry for Mrs. Brown. She was ashamed of the feeling. She knew that Mrs. Campbell did not have it. Hurrying to keep pace with that furious lady's haste down the street, Rose was overwhelmed with shame and confusion. The whole affair was like a splash of mud upon her. Her cheeks were red, and she could not make herself meet Mrs. Campbell's eyes.

Even when they were on the streetcar, safely away from it all, her awkwardness increased. Mrs. Campbell herself was a little disconcerted then. She looked at Rose, at the bulging telescope-bag, the shabby shoes, and the faded sailor hat, and Rose felt the gaze like a burn. She knew that Mrs. Campbell was wondering what on earth to do with her.

Pride and helplessness and shame choked her. She tried to respond to Mrs. Campbell's efforts at conversation, but she could not, though she knew that her failure made Mrs. Campbell think her sullen. Her rescuer's impatient tone was cutting her like the lash of a whip before they got off the car.

Mrs. Campbell lived in splendor in a two-story white house on a quiet street. The smoothness of the well-kept lawns, the immaculate propriety of the swept cement walks, cried out against Rose's shabbiness. She had never been so aware of it. When she was seated in Mrs.

Campbell's parlor, oppressed by the velvet upholstery and the piano and the bead portieres, she tried to hide her feet beneath the chair and did not know what to do with her hands.

She answered Mrs. Campbell's questions because she had to, but she felt that the last coverings of reticence and self-respect were being torn from her. Mrs. Campbell offered only one word of advice.

"The thing for you to do is to go home."

"No," Rose said. "I—I can't do that."

Mrs. Campbell looked at her curiously, and again the red flamed in Rose's cheeks. She could not discuss the renewed and increased mortgage on the farm, the money she owed her parents.

"Well, you can stay here a few days."

She lugged the telescope-bag up the stairs, the wooden steps of which shone like glass. Mrs. Campbell showed her a room at the end of the hall. A mass of things filled it; children's toys, old baskets, a broken chair. It was like the closets at home, but larger. It was large enough to hold a narrow white iron bed, a wash-stand, and a chair, and still leave room to swing the door open. These things appeared when Mrs. Campbell had dragged out the others.

Watching her swift, efficient motions in silence, Rose tried again to feel gratitude. But the fact that Mrs. Campbell expected it made it impossible. She could only stand awkwardly, longing for the moment when she would be alone. When at last Mrs. Campbell went downstairs she shut the door quickly and softly. She wanted to fling herself on the sagging bed and cry, but she did not. She stood with clenched hands, looking into the small, blurred mirror over the washstand. A white, tense face looked back at her with burning eyes. She said to it, "You're going to do something, do you hear? You're going to do something quick!"

Although she did not know what she could do, she could keep her self-control by telling herself that she would do something.

Some time later she heard the shouts of children and the clatter of pans in the kitchen below. It was almost supper-time. She took a cinnamon roll from the paper sack in her bag, but she could not eat it. She was looking at it when Mrs. Campbell called up the back stairs, "Miss Wilder! Come to supper."

She braced herself and went down. It was a good supper, but she could not eat very much. Mr. Campbell sat at the head of the table, a stern-looking man who said little except to speak sharply to the children when they were too noisy. There were two children, a girl of nine and a younger boy in a sailor suit. They looked curiously at Rose and did not reply when she tried to talk to them. She perceived that they had been told to leave her alone.

When she timidly offered to help with the dishes after supper Mrs. Campbell told her that she did not need any help. Her tone was not unkind, but Rose felt the rebuff, and fearing she would cry, she went quickly upstairs.

She looked at Paul's picture for some time before she put it back into her bag where she thought Mrs. Campbell would not see it. Then, sitting on the edge of the bed under a flickering gas-jet, she wrote him a long letter. She told him that she had moved, and in describing the street, the beautiful house, the furniture in the parlor, she drew such a picture of comfort and happiness that its reflection warmed her somewhat. It was a beautiful letter, she thought, reading it over several times before she carefully turned out the gas and went to bed.

Early in the morning she went to the telegraph-office and pleaded again for a job. Mr. Roberts, the manager, was very friendly, talking to her for some time and patting her hand in a manner which she thought fatherly and found comforting. He told her to come back. He might do something.

She went back every morning for a week, and often in the afternoons. The rest of the time she wandered in the streets or sat on a bench in the park. She felt under such obligations when she ate Mrs. Campbell's food that several times she did not return to the house until after dark, when supper would be finished. She had to ring the door bell, for the front door was kept locked, and each time Mrs. Campbell asked her sharply where she had been. She always answered truthfully.

By the end of the week Mr. Roberts had made a place for her in the office as a clerk. Her wages would be five dollars a week. When she hurried home that afternoon, eager to tell Mrs. Campbell the happy news, there was a letter waiting for her, propped on the hall table. It was from her mother. Mrs. Campbell had written to her, and she was horrified and alarmed.

> Your father says he is heartsick for you and I blame myself for ever letting you go all alone. You have a good home to come back to even if it isn't very fine, and don't worry about the money, short as we are of cash this winter, your father won't say a word. Just you come right away.
>
> Lovingly,
> Your Mother

Rose hated Mrs. Campbell. What right had that woman to worry her mother? Her anger when she read her mother's letter was obscurely a relief. The compulsion to feel gratitude toward Mrs. Campbell was lifted from her.

Rose could get along all right by herself, and she wrote

her mother that she could. She had a job at last. She did not mention the wages; she said only that she had a job and her mother was not to worry. She would be making more money soon and could send some home. When she finished the letter she hastened to drop it in the corner mail-box.

Running back to the house, she met Mrs. Campbell returning from a sewing-circle meeting. Mrs. Campbell was neatly hatted and gloved, and the expression in her pale blue eyes behind the dotted veil suddenly made Rose realize how blow-away she looked, bare-headed, her loosened hair ruffled by the breeze, her blouse sagging under her arms. She stood awkwardly self-conscious while Mrs. Campbell unlocked the front door.

"Did you get your mother's letter?"

"Yes. I got it."

"Well, what did she say?"

Rose did not answer that.

"I got a job," she said. Her breath came quickly.

"You have? What kind of job?"

Rose told her. They were in the hall now, standing by the golden-oak hat-rack at the foot of the stairs. The children watched, wide-eyed, in the parlor door.

Perplexity and disgust struggled on Mrs. Campbell's face.

"You think you're going to live in Sacramento on five dollars a week?"

"I'm going to. I've got to. I'll manage somehow. I won't go home!" Rose cried, confronting Mrs. Campbell like an antagonist.

"Oh, I don't doubt you'll *manage!*" Mrs. Campbell said cuttingly. She went down the hall, and the slam of the dining-room door shouted that she washed her hands of the whole affair.

She came up the back stairs half an hour later. Rose was sitting on the bed, her bag packed, trying to plan what to do. She had only the five dollars. It would be two weeks before she could get more money from the office. Mrs. Campbell opened the door without knocking.

"I'm going to talk this over with you," she said, patient firmness in her tone. "Don't you realize you can't get a decent room and anything to eat for five dollars a week? Do you think it's right to expect your folks to support you, poor as they are? It isn't—"

"I don't expect them to!" Rose cried.

"As though you didn't have a good home to go back to," Mrs. Campbell conveyed subtly that a well-bred girl did not interrupt while an older woman was speaking. "Now be reasonable about this."

"I won't go back," Rose said. She lifted miserable eyes to Mrs. Campbell's, and the expression she saw there reminded her of a horse with his ears laid back.

"Then you've decided, I suppose, where you *are* going?"

"No, I don't know. Can you tell me where to begin to look for a nice room that I can live in on my wages?"

Mrs. Campbell exclaimed impatiently. Her almost ruthless capability in dealing with situations did not prepare her to meet gracefully one that she could not handle. Her voice grew colder, and the smooth fair cheeks reddened while she continued to talk. Her arguments, her grudging attempts at persuasion, her final outburst of unconcealed anger, were futile. Rose would not go home. She meant to keep her job and to live on the wages.

"Well, then I guess you'll have to stay here. I can't turn you out on the streets."

"How much would you charge for the room?" said Rose.

"Charge!"

Rose flushed again at the scorn in the word. "I couldn't stay unless I paid you something. I'd have to do that."

"Well, of all the ungrateful!"

Tears came into Rose's eyes. She knew Mrs. Campbell meant well, and though she did not like her, she wished to thank her. But she did not know how to do it without yielding somewhat to the implacable force of the older woman. She could only repeat doggedly that she must pay for the room.

She was left shaken, but with a sense of victory emphasized by Mrs. Campbell's inarticulate exclamation as she went out. It was arranged that Rose should pay five dollars a month for the room.

But the bitterness of living in that house, on terms which she felt were charity, increased daily. She tried to make as little trouble as possible, stealing in at the back door so that no one would have to answer her ring, making her bed neatly, and slipping out early so that she would not meet any of the family. She spent her evenings at the office or at the library, where she could forget herself in books and in writing long letters. For some inexplicable reason this seemed to exasperate Mrs. Campbell, who inquired where she had been and did not hide a belief that her replies were lies. Rose felt like a suspected criminal. She would have left the house if she could have found another room that she could afford.

It was only at the office that she could breathe freely. She worked from eight in the morning to six at night, and then until the office closed at nine o'clock she could practice on the telegraph instrument behind the tables where the real wires came in. She worked hard at it, for at last she was on the road to the little station where she would work with Paul. Mr. Roberts was very kind. Often he came behind the screen where she was studying and talked to her for a long time. He was surprised at first by her working so hard. He seemed to think she had not meant to do it. But his manner was so warmly friendly that one day when he took her hand, saying, "What's the big idea, little girl—keeping me off like this?" she told him about everything but Paul. She told him, shamefaced, about Mr. Weeks' drinking, and that she did not know what she would have done if she had not got the job. She was very grateful to him and tried to tell him so.

He said drily not to bother about that, and she felt that she had offended him. Perhaps her story had sounded as if she were begging for more money, she thought with burning cheeks. For several days he gave her a great deal of hard work to do and was cross when she made mistakes. She did her best, trying hard to please him, and he was soon very friendly again.

His was the only friendliness she found to warm her shivering spirit, and she became daily more grateful to him for it. Though she was puzzled by his displays of affectionate interest in her and his sudden cold withdrawals when she eagerly thanked him, this was only part of the bewildering atmosphere of the office, in which she felt many undercurrents that she could not understand.

The young operator with the green eye-shade, for instance, always regarded her with a cynical and slightly amused eye, which she resented without knowing why. When she laid messages beside his key, he covered her hand with his if he could, and sometimes when she sat working he came and put his hand on her shoulder. She was always angry, for she felt contempt in his attitude toward her, but she did not know how to show her resentment without making too much of the incidents.

"Mr. McCormick, leave me alone!" she said impatiently. "I want to work."

He looked at her, grinning until she felt only that she hated him.

Much looking at life from the back-door keyhole of the

telegraph-operator's point of view had made him blasé and
wearily worldly-wise at twenty-two. He knew that every
pretty face was moulded on a skeleton, and was convinced
that all lives contained one. Only virtue could have
surprised him, and he could not have been convinced that
it existed. When he was on duty in the long, slow evenings,
Rose, practicing diligently behind her screen, heard him
singing thoughtfully:

> Life's a funny proposition after all;
> Just why we're here and what it's all about,
> It's a problem that has driven many brainy men to
> drink,
> It's a problem that they've never figured out.

Life seemed simple enough to Rose. She would be a
telegraph-operator soon, earning as much as fifty dollars a
month. She could repay the hundred dollars then, buy
some new clothes, and have plenty to eat. She would try to
get a job at the Ripley station, always in the back of her
mind was the thought of Paul, and she planned the
furnishing of housekeeping rooms, and thought of making
curtains and embroidering centerpieces.

It was spring when he wrote that he was coming to spend
a day in Sacramento. He was going to Mansfield to help
his mother move to Ripley. On the way he would stop and
see Rose.

Rose, in happy excitement, thought of her clothes. She
must have something new to wear when they met. Paul
must see in the first glance how much she had changed,
how much she had improved. She had not been able to
save anything, but she must, she must have new clothes.
Two days of worried planning brought her courage to the
point of approaching Mr. Roberts and asking him for her

next month's salary in advance. Next month's food was a problem she could meet later. Mr. Roberts was very kind about it.

"Money? Of course!" he said. He took a bill from his own pocket-book. "We'll have to see about your getting more pretty soon." Her heart leaped. He put the bill in her palm, closing his hand around hers. "Going to be good to me if I do?"

"Oh, I'd do anything in the world I could for you," she said, looking at him gratefully. "Thank you ever so much." His look struck her as odd, but a customer came in at that moment, and in taking the message she forgot about it.

She went out at noon and bought a white pleated voile skirt for five dollars, a China-silk waist for three-ninety-five and a white straw sailor hat. And that afternoon McCormick, with his cynical smile, handed her a note that had come over the wire for her. "Arrive eight ten Sunday morning. Meet me. Paul."

She was so radiantly self-absorbed all the afternoon that she hardly saw the thundercloud gathering in Mr. Roberts' eyes, and she went back to her room that evening so confidently happy that she rang the door-bell without her usual qualm. Mrs. Campbell's lips were drawn into a tight, thin line.

"There are some packages for you," she said.

"Yes, I know. I bought some clothes. Thank you for taking them in," said Rose. She felt friendly even toward Mrs. Campbell. "A white voile skirt, and a silk waist, and a hat. Would you like to see them?"

"No, *thank* you!" said Mrs. Campbell, icily. Going up the stairs, Rose heard her speaking to her husband. " 'I bought some clothes,' she says, bold as brass. Clothes!"

Rose wondered, hurt, how people could be so unkind. She knew that the clothes were an extravagance, but she did want them so badly, for Paul, and it seemed to her that she had worked hard enough to deserve them. Besides, Mr. Roberts had said that she might get a raise.

She was dressed and creeping noiselessly out of the house at seven o'clock the next morning. The spring dawn was coming rosily into the city after a night of rain; the odor of the freshly washed lawns and flower-beds was delicious, and birds sang in the trees. The flavor of the cool, sweet air and the warmth of the sunshine mingled with her joyful sense of youth and coming happiness. She looked very well, she thought, watching her slim white reflection in the shop windows.

Chapter 6

When the train pulled into the big, dingy station Rose had been waiting for some time, her pulses fluttering with excitement. But her self-confidence deserted her when she saw the crowds pouring from the cars. She shrank back into the waiting-room doorway; and she saw Paul before his eager eyes found her.

It was a shock to find that he had changed, too. Something boyish was gone from his face, and his self-confident walk, his prosperous appearance in a new suit, gave her the chill sensation that she was about to meet a stranger. She braced herself for the effort, and when they shook hands she felt that hers was cold.

"You're looking well," she said shyly.

"Well, so are you," he answered. They walked down the platform together, and she saw that he carried a new suitcase, and that even his shoes were new and shining. However, these details were somewhat offset by her perception that he was feeling awkward, too.

"Where shall we go?" They hesitated, looking at each other, and in their smile the strangeness vanished.

"I don't care. Anywhere, if you're along," he said. "Oh, Rose, it sure is great to see you again! You look like a million dollars, too." His approving eye was upon her new clothes.

"I'm glad you like them," she said, radiant. "That's an awfully nice suit, Paul." Happiness came back to her in a flood and putting out her hand, she picked a bit of thread from his dear sleeve. "Well, where shall we go?"

"We'll get something to eat first," he said practically. "I'm about starved, aren't you?" She had not thought of eating.

They breakfasted in a little restaurant on waffles and sausages and coffee. The hot food was delicious, and the waiter in the soiled white apron grinned understandingly while he served them. Paul gave him fifteen cents, in an offhand manner, and she thrilled at his careless prodigality and his air of knowing his way about.

The whole long day lay before them, bright with limitless possibilities. They left the suitcase with the cashier of the restaurant and walked slowly down the street, embarrassed by the riches of time that were theirs. Rose suggested that they walk awhile in the capitol grounds; she had supposed they would do that, and perhaps in the afternoon enjoy a car-ride to Oak Park. But Paul dismissed these simple pleasures with a word.

"Nothing like that," he said. "I want a real celebration, a regular blow-out. I've been saving up for it a long time." He struggled with his conscience. "It won't do any harm to miss church one Sunday. Let's take a boat down the river."

"Oh, Paul!" She was dazzled. "But won't it be awfully expensive?"

"I don't care how much it costs," he replied recklessly. "Come on. It'll be fun."

They went down the shabby streets toward the river, and even the dingy tenements and broken sidewalks of the Japanese quarter seemed to them to have a holiday air.

They laughed about the queer little shops and the restaurant windows, where electric lights still burned in the clear daylight over pallid pies and strange-looking cakes. Rose must stop to speak to the straight-haired, flat-faced Japanese babies who sat stolidly on the curbs, looking at her with enigmatic, slant eyes, and she saw romance in the groups of tall Hindu laborers, with their bearded, black faces and gaily colored turbans.

It was like going into a foreign land together, she said, and even Paul was momentarily caught by the enchantment she saw in it all, though he did not conceal his detestation of these foreigners. "We're going to see to it we don't have them in our town," he said, already with the air of a proprietor in Ripley.

"Now this is more like it!" he exclaimed when he had helped Rose across the gang-plank and deposited her safely on the deck of the steamer. Rose, pressing his arm with her fingers, was too happy to speak. The boat was filling with people in holiday clothes; everywhere about her was the exciting stir of departure, calls, commands, the thump of boxes being loaded on the deck below. A whistle sounded hoarsely, the engines were starting, sending a thrill through the very planks beneath her feet.

"We'd better get a good place up in front," said Paul. He took her through the magnificence of a large room furnished with velvet chairs, past a glimpse of shining white tables and white-clad waiters, to a seat whence they could gaze down the yellow river. She was overawed by his ease and assurance. She looked at him with an admiration which she would not allow to lessen even when the boat edged out into the stream and, turning, revealed that he had led her to the stern deck.

Her enthusiastic suggestion that they explore the boat aided Paul's attempt to conceal his chagrin, and she listened enthralled to his explanations of all they saw. He estimated the price of the crates of vegetables and chickens piled on the lower deck, on their way to the city from the upper river farms. It was his elaborate description of the engines that caught the attention of a grimy engineer who had emerged from the noisy depths for a breath of air, and the engineer, turning on them a quizzically friendly gaze, was easily persuaded to take them into the engine-room.

Rose could not understand his explanations, but she was interested because Paul was, and found her own thrill in the discovery of a dim tank half filled with flopping fish, scooped from the river and flung there by the paddle wheel. "We take 'em home and eat 'em, miss," said the engineer, and she pictured their cool lives in the green river, and the city supper tables at which they would be eaten.

It was a disappointment to find, when they returned again to the upper decks, that they could see nothing but green levee banks on each side of the river. But this led to an even more exciting discovery, for venturesomely climbing a slender iron ladder they saw beyond the western levee an astounding and incredible stretch of water where land should be. Their amazement emboldened Paul to tap on the glass wall of a small room beside them, in which they saw an old man peacefully smoking his pipe. He proved to be the pilot, who explained that it was flood water they saw, and who let them squeeze into his tiny quarters and stay while he told long talks of early days on the river, of floods in which whole settlements were swept away at night, of women and children rescued from floating roofs, of cows found drowned in treetops, and droves of hogs that cut their own throats with their hoofs while swimming. Listening to him while the boat slowly chugged down the curves of the sunlit river, Rose felt the romance of living, the color of all the millions of obscure lives in the world.

"Isn't everything interesting!" she cried, giving Paul's

arm an excited little squeeze as they walked along the main deck again. "Oh, I'd like to live all the lives that ever were lived! Think of those women and the miners and people in cities and everything!"

"I expect you'd find it pretty inconvenient before you got through," Paul said. "Gee, you're awfully pretty, Rose," he added irrelevantly, and they forgot everything except that they were together.

They had to get off at Lancaster in order to catch the late afternoon boat back to Sacramento. There was just time to eat on board, Paul said, and overruling her flurried protests he led her into the white-painted dining room. The smooth linen, the shining silver, and the imposing waiters confused her; she was able to see nothing but the prices on the elaborate menu-cards, and they were terrifying. Paul himself was startled by them, and she could see worried calculation in his eyes. She felt that she should pay her share; she was working, too, and earning money. The memory of the office, the advance she had drawn on her wages, her uncomfortable existence in Mrs. Campbell's house, passed through her mind like a shadow. But it was gone in an instant, and she sat happily at the white table, eating small delicious sandwiches and drinking milk, smiling across immaculate linen at Paul. For a moment she played with the fancy that it was a honeymoon trip, and a thrill ran along her nerves.

They were at Lancaster before they knew it. There was a moment of flurried haste, and they stood on the levee, watching the boat push off and disappear beyond a wall of willows. A few loungers looked at them with expressionless eyes, and brought forth the information that the afternoon boat was late. It might be along about five o'clock, they thought.

"Well, that'll get us back in time for my train," Paul decided. "Let's look around a little."

The levee road was a tunnel of willow-boughs, floored with soft sand in which their feet made no sound. They walked in an enchanted stillness, through pale light, green as sea water, drowsy, warm, and scented with the breath of unseen flowers. Through the thin wall of leaves they caught glimpses of the broad river, the yellow waves of which gave back the color of the sky in flashes of metallic blue. And suddenly, stepping out of the perfumed shadow, they saw the orchards. A sea of petals, fragile, translucent, unearthly as waves of pure rosy light, rippled at their feet.

The loveliness of it filled Rose's eyes with tears. "Oh!" she said, softly. "Oh, Paul!" Her hand went out blindly toward him. One more breath of magic would make the moment perfect. She did not know what she wanted, but her whole being was longing for it. "Oh, Paul!"

"Pears! Hundreds of acres, Rose," he cried. "They're the tops of trees! We're looking down at 'em! Look at the river. Why, the land's fifteen feet below water-level. Did you ever see anything like it?" Excitement shook his voice. "There must be a way to get down there. I want to see it!" He almost ran along the edge of the levee; Rose had to hurry to keep beside him. She did not know why she should be hurt because Paul was interested in the orchards. She was the first to laugh about going downstairs to farm when they found the wooden steps on the side of the levee.

But she felt rebuffed and almost resentful. She listened abstractedly to Paul's talk about irrigation and the soil. He crumbled handfuls of it between his fingers while they walked between the orchard rows, and his opinion led to a monologue on the soil around Ripley and the fight the farmers were making to get water on it. He was conservative about the project; it might pay, and it might not. But if it did, a man who bought some cheap land now would make a good thing out of it. It occurred to her suddenly to wonder about the girls in Ripley. There must be some;

Paul had never written about them. She thought about it for some time before she was able to bring the talk to the point where she could ask about them.

"Girls?" Paul said. "Sure there are. I don't pay much attention to them, though. I see them in church, and they're at the Aid Society suppers, of course. They seem pretty foolish to me. Why, I never noticed whether they were pretty, or not." Enlightenment dawned upon him. "I'll tell you; they don't seem to talk about anything much. You're the only girl I ever knew that I could really talk to. I've been awfully lonesome, thinking about you."

"Really truly?" she said, looking up at him. The sunlight fell across her white dress, and stray pink petals fluttered slowly downward around her. "Have you really been lonesome for me, too?" She swayed toward him, ever so little, and he put his arms around her.

He did love her. A great contentment flowed through her. To be in his arms again was to be safe and rested and warm after ages of racking effort in the cold. He was thinking only of her now. His arms crushed her against him; she felt the roughness of his coat under her cheek. He was stammering love-words, kissing her hair, her cheeks, her lips.

"Oh, Paul, I love you, I love you, I love you!" she said, her arms around his neck.

Much later they found a little nook under the willows on the levee bank and sat there with the river rippling at their feet, his arm around her, her head on his shoulder. They talked a little then. Paul told her again all about Ripley, but she did not mind. "When we're married—" said Paul, and the rest of the sentence did not matter.

"And I'm going to help you," Rose said. "Because I'm telegraphing now, too. I'll be earning as much—almost as much, as you do. We can live over the depot."

"We will not!" said Paul. "We'll have a house. I don't know that I'm crazy about my wife working."

"Oh, but I do want to help! A house would be nice. Oh, Paul, with rosebushes in the yard!"

"And a horse and buggy, so we can go riding Sunday afternoons."

"Besides, if I'm making money . . ."

"I know. We wouldn't have to wait so long. Of course there's mother. And I want to feel that I can support . . ."

She felt the magic departing.

"Never mind!" The tiniest of cuddling movements brought his arms tight around her again.

They were startled when they noticed the shadows under the trees. They had not dreamed it was so late. She smoothed her hair and pinned on her hat with trembling fingers, and they raced for the landing. The river was an empty stretch of dirty gray lapping dusky banks. There was no one at the landing.

"It must be way after five o'clock. I wish I had a watch. The boat couldn't have gone by without our seeing it!" The suggestion drained the color from their cheeks. They looked at each other with wide eyes. "It couldn't have possibly! Let's ask."

The little town was no more than half a dozen old wooden buildings facing the levee. A store, unlighted and locked, a harness shop, also locked, two dark warehouses, a saloon. She waited in the shadow of it while he went in to inquire. He came out almost immediately.

"No, the boat hasn't gone. They don't know when it'll get here."

They walked uncertainly back to the landing and stood gazing at the darkening river. "I suppose there's no knowing when it will get here? There's no other way of getting back?"

"No, there's no railroad. I *have* got you into a scrape!"

"It's all right. It wasn't your fault," she hastened to say.

They walked up and down, waiting. Darkness came slowly down upon them. The river breeze grew colder. Stars appeared.

"Chilly?"

"A little," she said through chattering teeth.

He took off his coat and wrapped it around her, despite her protests. They found a sheltered place on the bank and huddled together, shivering. A delicious sleepiness stole over her, and the lap-lap of the water, the whispering of the leaves, the warmth of Paul's shoulder under her cheek, all became like a dream.

"Comfortable, dear?"

"Mmmmmhuh," she murmured. "You?"

"You bet your life!" She roused a little to meet his kiss. The night became dreamlike again.

"Rose?"

"What?"

"Seems to me we've been here a long time. What'll we do? We can't stay here till morning."

"I don't know why not. All night under the stars . . ."

"But listen. What if the boat comes by and doesn't stop? There isn't any light."

She sat up then, rubbing the drowsiness from her eyes.

"Well, let's make a fire. Got any matches?"

He always carried them, to light the switch-lamps in Ripley. They hunted dry branches and driftwood and coaxed a flickering blaze alive. "It's like being stranded on a desert island!" she laughed. His eyes adored her, crouching with disheveled hair in the leaping yellow light. "You're certainly game," he said. "I think you're the pluckiest girl in the world. And when I think what a fool I was to get you into this!"

There came like an echo down the river the hoarse

whistle of the boat. A moment later it was upon them, looming white and gigantic, its lights cutting swaths in the darkness as it edged in to the landing. Struggling to straighten her hat, to tuck up her hair, to brush the sand from her skirt, Rose stumbled aboard with Paul's hand steadying her.

The blaze of the salon lights hurt their eyes, but warmth and security relaxed tired muscles. The room was empty, its carpet swept, the velvet chairs neatly in place.

"Funny, I thought there'd be a lot of passengers," Paul wondered aloud. He found a cushion, tucked it behind Rose's head, and sat down beside her. "Well, we're all right now. We'll be in Sacramento pretty soon."

"Don't let's think about it," she said with quivering lips. "I hate to have it all end, such a lovely day. It'll be such a long time."

He held her hand tightly.

"Not so awfully long. I'm not going to stand for it." He spoke firmly, but his eyes were troubled. She did not answer, and they sat thinking about the future while the boat jolted on toward the moment of their parting.

"Damn being poor!" The word startled her as a blow would have done. Paul, so sincerely and humbly a church member—Paul swearing! He went on without a pause. "If I had a little money, if I only had a little money! What right has it got to make such a difference? Oh, Rose, you don't know how I want you!"

"Paul, Paul dear, you mustn't!" Her hand was crushed against his face, his shoulders shook. She drew his dear, tousled head against her shoulder.

After a moment he pushed away from her and got up. She let him go, shielding his embarrassment even from her own eyes. "I seem to be making a fool of myself generally," he said shakily. He walked about the room, looking with an appearance of interest at the pictures on the walls. "It's funny there aren't more people on board," he said conversationally after a while. "Well, I guess I'll go see what time we get in." He came back five minutes later, an odd expression on his face.

"Look, Rose," he said gruffly. "We won't get in for hours. Something wrong with the engines. They're only making half time. I don't know why I didn't think of it before. You've got to work tomorrow and all. The man suggested . . ."

"Well, for goodness' sake, suggested what?"

"Everybody else has berths," he said. "You better let me get you one, because there's no sense in your sitting up all night. There's no knowing when we'll get in."

"But, Paul, I hate to have you spend so much. I could sleep a little right here." A vision of the office went through her mind, and she saw herself, sleepy-eyed, struggling to get messages into the right envelopes and trying to manage the unmanageable messenger-boys. She was tired. But it would be awfully expensive, no doubt. "And besides, I'd rather stay here with you," she said.

"So would I. But we might as well be sensible. You've got to work, and I'd probably go to sleep, too. Come on, let's see how much it is, anyhow."

They found the right place after wandering twice around the boat. A weary man sat behind the half-door, adding up a column of figures. "Berths? Sure. Outside, of course. One left. Dollar and a half." His expectation brought the money, as if automatically, from Paul's pocket. He came out, yawning, a key with a dangling tag in his hand. "This way."

They followed him down the corridor. Matters seemed to be taken from their hands. He stepped out on the dark deck.

"Careful there, better give your wife a hand over those ropes," he cautioned over his shoulder, and they heard the sound of a key in a lock. An oblong of light appeared; he stepped out again to let them pass him. They went in. "There's towels. Everything all right, I guess," he said cheerfully. "Good night."

Their eyes met for one horrified second. Embarrassment covered them both like a flame. "Rose! You don't think—?" They swayed uncertainly in the narrow space between berths and wash-stand. Did the boat jolt so or was it the beating of her heart?

"Paul, did you hear? How could—?"

"I guess I better go now," he said. He fumbled with the door. "Good night."

"Good night." She felt suddenly forlorn. But he was not gone. "Rose? It might be true. We might be married! Rose?"

She clung to him.

"We can't! We couldn't! Oh, Paul, oh, I love you so."

"We can be married—we will be—just as soon as we get to Sacramento." His kisses smothered her. "The very first thing in the morning! We'll manage somehow. Rose, what's the matter? Look at me. Darling!"

"We can't," she gasped. "I'd be spoiling everything for you. Your mother and me and everything on your hands and you're just getting started. You'd hate me after a while. No, no, no!"

They stumbled apart.

"What am I saying?" he said hoarsely, and she turned away from him, hiding her face.

A rush of cold moist air blew in upon her from the open doorway. He was gone. She got the door shut, and sat down on the edge of the berth. A cool breeze flowed in like water through the shutters of the windows; she felt the throbbing of the engines. Even through her closed lids she could not bear the light, and after a while she turned it out, trembling, and lay open-eyed in the darkness.

The stopping of the boat struck her aching nerves like a blow. She sat up, neither asleep nor awake, pushing her hair back from a face that seemed sodden and lifeless. A pale twilight filled the stateroom. She smoothed her hair, straightened her crumpled dress as well as she could, and went out on the deck. The boat lay at the Sacramento landing.

A few feet away Paul was leaning upon the railing, his face pale and haggard in the cold light. As she went toward him the events of the night danced fantastically through her brain, as grotesque and feverish as images in a dream.

"You don't hate me, do you, Rose?" he pleaded hopelessly.

"Of course not," she said. Through her weariness she felt a stirring of pity. For the first time in her life she told herself to smile, and did it. "We'd better be getting off, hadn't we?"

The grayness of dawn was in the air, paling the street lights. A few workmen passed them, plodding stolidly, carrying lunch-pails and tools; a baker's wagon rattled by, awakening loud echoes. She tried to comfort Paul, whose talk was one long self-reproach.

He hoped she would not get into a row with the folks where she stayed. If she did, she must let him know; he wouldn't stand for anything like that. She could reach him in Mansfield until he came back again on his way home. He hadn't thought he could stop on the way, but he would. He'd be worried about her until he saw her again and was sure everything was all right. He had been an awful boob not to be sure about the boat; he'd never forgive himself if . . .

"What is it?" he broke off. She had turned to look after a young man who passed them. The motion was almost automatic; she had hardly seen the man and not until he was past did her tired mind register an impression of a cynical smile.

"Nothing," she said. It had been McCormick. But it would require too much effort to talk about him.

The blinds of Mrs. Campbell's house were still down when they reached it. The tight roll of the morning paper lay on the porch. She would have to ring, of course, to get in. They faced each other on the damp cement walk, the freshness of the dewy lawns about them.

"Well, goodbye."

"Goodbye." They felt constrained in the daylight, under the blank stare of the windows. Their hands clung. "You really aren't mad at me, Rose, about anything?"

"Of course I'm not. Nothing's happened that wasn't as much my fault as it was yours."

"You'll let me know if—if there's any trouble?"

She promised, though she had no intention of bothering him with her problems. It was not his fault that the boat was late, and she had gone as gladly as he. "Don't worry about it; I'll be all right. Goodbye, dear."

"Goodbye, Rose." Still their fingers clung together. She felt a rush of tenderness toward him.

"Don't look so worried, dear!" Quickly, daringly, she leaned toward him and brushed a butterfly's wing of a kiss upon his cheek. Then, embarrassed, she ran up the steps.

Rose watched Paul's strong body until it turned the corner. Then she rang the bell. There was time for the momentary glow to depart, leaving her weak and chilly, before Mrs. Campbell opened the door. She said nothing. Her eyes, her tight lips, her manner of drawing her dressing-gown back from Rose's approach, spoke her thoughts. Explanations would be met with scornful unbelief.

Rose held her head high and countered silence with silence. But before she reached her room she heard Mrs. Campbell's voice, high-pitched and cutting, speaking to her husband.

"Brazen as you please! You're right. The only thing to

do's to put her out of this house before we have a scandal on our hands. That's what I get for taking her in out of charity!"

Rose shut her door softly. She would leave the house that very day. The battered alarm clock pointed to half-past five. Three hours before she could do anything. She undressed mechanically, half-formed plans rushing through her mind. No money, next month's wages spent for these crumpled clothes. She could telegraph her mother, but she must not alarm her. Why hadn't she thought of borrowing something from Paul? There was Mr. Roberts, but she could never make up more money. Perhaps he would advance the raise he had promised. Her brain was working with hectic rapidity. She saw in flashes rooming houses, the office, Mr. Roberts. She thought out every detail of long conversations, heard her own voice explaining, arguing, promising, thanking.

Chapter 7

Rose awoke with a start at the sound of the alarm. Her sleep had not refreshed her. Her body felt wooden, and there was a gritty sensation behind her eyes. Dressing and hurrying to the office was like a nightmare in which a tremendous effort accomplishes nothing. The office routine steadied her. She booked the night messages, laying wet tissue paper over them, running them through the copying machine, addressing their envelopes, sending out messenger-boys, settling their disputes over long routes. Everything was as usual; the sunshine streamed in through the plate-glass front of the office; customers came and went; the telephone rang; the instruments clicked. Her holiday was gone as if she had dreamed it. There remained only the recurring sting of Mrs. Campbell's words, and a determination to leave her house.

She tried several times to talk to Mr. Roberts. But he was in a black mood. He walked past her without saying good-morning, and over the question of a delayed message his voice snapped like a whiplash. She saw that some obscure fury was working in him and that he would grant no favors until it had worn itself out. Perhaps he would be in a better humor later. She must ask him for some money before night.

In the lull just before noon she sat at her table behind the screen, her head on her arms. She did not feel like working at the instrument. Mr. McCormick was lounging against the front counter, talking to Mr. Roberts, who sat at his desk. They would take care of any customers; for a moment she could rest and try to think.

"Miss Wilder!"

"Yes, sir!" She leaped to her feet. Mr. Roberts' tone was dangerous. Had she forgotten a message?

"I'd like to show you the substitute connection to the batteries. Come with me."

She followed him gingerly down the stairway to the basement. The batteries stood in great rows on racks of shelves, big glass jars rimmed with poisonous-looking green and yellow stains, filled with discolored water and pieces of rotting metal. A failing light bulb illuminated their dusty ranks, and dimly showed black beams and cobwebs overhead.

"It's very good of you to take so much trouble," she began gratefully.

"Cut that out! How long're you going to think you're making a damn fool of me?" Mr. Roberts turned on her suddenly a face that terrified her. Words choked in his throat. He caught her wrist, and she felt his whole body shaking. "You—you—damned little—" The rows of glass jars spun around her. She hardly understood the words he flung at her. "Coming here with your big eyes, playing me for all you're worth, acting innocent! D'you think you've fooled me a minute? D'you think I haven't seen through your little game? How long d'you think I'm going to stand for it? Dammit!"

"Let me go," she said, panting.

She steadied herself against the end of a rack, where his furious gesture flung her. They faced each other in the close space, breathing hard. "I don't know what you mean," she said. Her world was going to pieces under her feet.

"You know damn well what I mean. Don't keep on lying to me. You can't put it over. I know where you were last night." His face was contorted again. "Yes, and all the other nights, all the time you've been kidding yourself you were making a fool of me. I know all about it. Get that? I know what you were before I ever gave you a job. What d'you suppose I gave it to you for? So you could run around on the outside, laughing at me?"

"Wait—oh, please—"

"I've done all the listening to you I'm going to do. You're going to do something besides talk from now on. I'm not a boy you can twist around your finger. I don't care how cute you are."

"I don't want to. I only want to get away," she said. She still faced him, for she could not hide her face without taking her eyes from him, and she was afraid to do that. When the silence continued she began to drop into it small disjointed phrases. "I didn't know, I thought you were so good to me. We couldn't help the boat being late. Please, please, just let me go away. I was only trying to learn the telegraph. I thought I was doing so well."

She felt, then, that he was no longer angry, and turning against the cobwebbed boards, she covered her face with her arms and cried. She hated herself for doing it; but she could not help it. Every instant she tried to stop, and very soon she was able to do so. When she lifted her head Mr. Roberts was gone.

She waited a while among the uncaring battery jars, steadying herself and wiping her face with her handkerchief. When she forced herself to climb up into the daylight again there was no one in the office but McCormick, who sat at the San Francisco wire, gazing into space, whistling "Life's a funny proposition after all," while the disregarded sounder clattered fretfully, calling him.

Of course she would leave the office. She put on her hat and did so at once, but when she was out in the sunlight with the eyes of passers-by upon her, she could do nothing but writhe among her thoughts like a flayed thing among nettles. The side streets were better than the others, for there fewer people could see her. If it were only night, so she could crawl unobserved into some corner and die.

It was a long time before Rose realized that her body was aching and that she was limping on painful feet. She had reached a street in some residence subdivision, where cement sidewalks ran through tangles of last year's weeds, and little cottages stood forlornly at long intervals. She stumbled over an expanse of dry stubble and green grass and sat down. She could not suffer any more. It was good to sit in the warm sunshine, to be alone. Life was vile. She shrank from it with sick loathing. She had been so hurt that she no longer felt pain, but her soul was nauseated.

There was no refuge into which she could crawl. There was no time to heal her bruises, no one to help her bear them. The afternoon was almost gone. At the house there was Mrs. Campbell, at the office. . . . She could get more money from her mother and go home to stay. She owed her family a hundred dollars: months of privation and heart-breaking work. She could not shudder away from the hideousness of life at such a cost to others. Somehow she must find strength in herself to stand up, to go on, to do something.

Mr. Roberts' recommendation was necessary before she could get another telegraph job. She did not know how to do anything else. She owed him ten dollars, which must be paid. Paul—warm blood rose in her cheeks when her thoughts touched him. She must face this thing alone.

In the depth of her mind Rose felt a hardness growing. All her finer sensibilities, hurt beyond bearing, were concealing themselves beneath a coarser hardihood. Her chin went up, her lips set, her eyes narrowed unconsciously.

After a long time she rose, brushing dead grass-stalks

from her skirt, and started back to town. A streetcar carried her there quickly. On the way she remembered that she should eat, and thought of Mrs. Brown. The half-punched meal-ticket was still in her purse. She had shivered at the thought of ever seeing Mrs. Brown again, and many times she had intended to throw away the bit of pasteboard, but she had not been able to do so because it represented food.

She got off the car at the corner nearest the little restaurant, and forced herself to its doors. It was closed and empty, and a "For Rent" sign was glued to the dirty window. Under her quick relief there was a sense of triumph. She had made herself go there, at least.

In a dairy-lunch she drank a cup of coffee and swallowed a sandwich. Then she went back to the telegraph office.

She held her head high and walked steadily, as she might have gone to her own execution. She felt that something within her was being crushed to death, some-thing clean and fine and sensitive, which must die before she could make herself face Mr. Roberts again. She opened the office door and went in.

Mr. Roberts was at one of the wires. McCormick, frowning, was booking messages at her high desk. She hung her hat in the cabinet and took the pen from his hand.

"Well, Miss Bright-eyes, welcome to our city!" he exclaimed in his usual manner, but she saw that he was nervous, disturbed by the sense of tension in the air.

"After this you're going to call me Miss Wilder," she said, folding a message into an envelope. She struck the bell for the next messenger-boy. Well, she had been able to do that.

It was harder to approach Mr. Roberts. Rose did not know whether she most shrank from him, despised him, or feared him, but her heart fluttered and she felt ill when he came through the railing into the office and sat down at his desk. She went over the day's bookings, and checked up the messenger books without seeing them, until her hatred of her cowardice grew into a kind of courage. Then she went over to his desk.

"Mr. Roberts," she said clearly. "I'm not any of the things you called me." Her cheeks, her forehead, even her neck, were burning painfully. "I'm a perfectly decent girl."

"Well, there's no use making such a fuss about it," he mumbled, searching among his papers for one which apparently was not there.

"I wouldn't stay, only I owe you ten dollars and I've got to have a job. You know that. It was all the truth I told you, about having to work. I've got to stay here—"

"How do you know I'm going to let you?" he said, stung.

"I'm a good clerk. You can't get another as good any cheaper." She found herself on the defensive and struck wildly. "You ought to anyway let me keep the job, to make up—"

"That'll do," he said harshly. Turning away from her he caught McCormick's eye, which dropped quickly to the message he was sending.

Rose had to face the crisis. Her mind whirled. Dared she . . . ?

She walked woodenly back to her desk, and shuffled the papers until she found the all-stations message that had come in the morning. Western Union in San Francisco needed immediately a night operator at the St. Francis hotel, would pay forty-five dollars a month.

CAN ARRIVE EIGHT P.M. TONIGHT
FOR PERMANENT DUTY
CALVIN ROBERTS WILL CONFIRM
EXPERIENCE AT SACRAMENTO OFFICE.

Her hand steely, her mind shaking, Rose walked to Mr. Roberts' desk and dropped both messages on it. She wanted to say, "Shall I send it?" but the words clogged together in her throat.

Mr. Roberts read them twice, and stared at the wall. He handed them back without looking at her and said, with an attempt at sarcasm, "I'll try to keep the office going without your assistance."

She had won. Hers was the next wire out; McCormick saw it and grinned. It startled her to find she was meeting it with a little twisted smile almost as cynical. What she wanted to do was to scream.

In the middle of the afternoon she was leaning on the front counter, watching people go by outside the plateglass windows and wondering what was the truth about them, when she felt McCormick's gaze upon her. He came a step closer, putting his elbow on the counter beside hers, and spoke confidentially. "Bryant at San Francisco just wired he'd meet the train and take you to the hotel. You know, you're darn plucky—I like you." He spoke meditatively, as if considering impersonally his sensations. "Made a killing at poker last night," he went on. When she did not answer, "There's no string tied to a little loan."

"Yes. I'll go now," she said, exhausted of feeling. "I think everything's in order. The Ramsey message was sent out twice."

She borrowed ten dollars from McCormick, promising to return it at the end of the month. She hardly resented his elaborately kissing the money good-by, and holding her hand when he gave it to her. But she spent twenty-five cents of it to send a message from the station to Paul, though McCormick would have sent it for her at no cost.

Part II

Chapter 8

Cooped in a narrow space at the end of a long corridor, Rose sat gazing at the life of a great San Francisco hotel. Every moment the color and glitter shifted under the brilliant light of mammoth chandeliers. Tall, gilded elevator-doors opened and closed; women passed, wrapped in satins and velvets, airy feathers in their shining hair; men in evening dress escorted them; bell-boys went by, carrying silver trays and calling unintelligibly, their voices rising above the continuous muffled stir and the faint sounds of music from the Blue Room.

Rose had choked the telegraph-sounder with a pencil, so that she might hear the music. But the tones of the violins came to her blurred by a low hum of voices, by the rustle of silks, by the soft movement of many feet on velvet carpets. Nothing was clear, simple, or distinct in the medley. Her ears were baffled, as her eyes were dazzled and her thoughts confused by a multiplicity of sensations. San Francisco was a whirlpool, an endless roaring circle, stupendous and dizzying.

This had been her impression of it on that first morning, when she struggled through the eddying crowds at the ferry building, lugging her telescope-bag with one hand and with the other trying to hold her hat in place against gusts of wind. Beneath the uproar of streetcar gongs, of huge wagons rumbling over the cobbles, of innumerable hurrying feet, whistles, bells, shouts, she had felt a great impersonal current, terrifying in its heedlessness of all but its own mighty swirl, and she had had the sensation of standing at the brink of a maelstrom.

After ten months the impression still remained. But now Rose seemed to have been drawn into the motionless vortex. The city roared around her, still incomprehensible, still driven by its own breathless speed, but in the heart of it she was alien and untouched. She had found nothing in it but loneliness.

Her first terrors had vanished, leaving her with a frustrated sense of having been ridiculous in having them. She had gathered her whole strength for a great effort, and she had found nothing to do. Far from lying in wait with nameless dangers and pitfalls for the unwary stranger, the city apparently did not know she was there.

At the main Western Union office Mr. Bryant had received her indifferently. He was a busy man; she was one detail of his routine work. He directed her to the St. Francis, asked her to report there at five o'clock, and, looking at her again, inquired whether she knew any one in San Francisco or had arranged for a place to live. Three minutes later he handed her over to a brisk young woman, who gave her an address and told her what car to take to reach it.

She had found a shabby two-story house on Gough Street with a discouraged palm in a tub on the front porch. A colorless woman showed her the room. It was a small, neat place under the eaves, furnished with an iron bed, a washstand, a chair, and a strip of rag carpet. The bathroom was on the lower floor, and the rent was two dollars and a half a week. Rose set down her bag with a sigh of relief.

Thus simply she found herself established in San Francisco. Her first venture into the St. Francis had been no more exciting. After a panic-stricken plunge into its magnificence she was accepted noncommitally by the day-operator, a pale girl with eye glasses, who was already putting on her hat. She turned over a few unsent messages, gave Rose the cash-box and rate-book, and departed.

Thereafter Rose met her daily, punctually at five o'clock, and saw her leave. Rose rather looked forward to the moment. It was pleasant to say, "Good evening," once a day to someone.

In the afternoon she walked about, looking at the city, and learned to know many of the streets by name. She discovered the public library and read a great deal. The library was also a pleasant place to spend Sundays, being less lonely than the crowded parks, and if the librarian were not too busy one might sometimes talk to her about a book.

The dragging of the days, as much as her need for more money, had driven her to asking for extra work at the main office. But here, too, she had been dropped into the machine and put down before her telegraph-key, with barely a hurried human touch. A beginner, rated at forty-five dollars, she replaced a seventy-five-dollar operator on a heavy wire, and the days became a nerve-straining tension of concentration on the clicking sounder at her ear, while the huge room with its hundreds of instruments and operators faded from her consciousness.

Released at four o'clock, she ate forlornly in a dairy lunchroom and hurried to the St. Francis. Here, at least, she could watch other people's lives. Gazing out at the changing crowd in the hotel corridor she let her imagination picture the romances, the adventures, at her fingertips. A man spoke cheerfully to the cigar-boy while he lighted his cigarette at the swinging light over the news stand counter. He was the center of a scandal that had filled the afternoon papers, and under her hand was the message he had sent to his wife, denying, appealing, swearing loyalty and love. A little, soft-eyed woman in clinging laces, stepping from the elevator to meet a plump man in evening dress, was there to put through a big mining deal with him. The ends of the intrigue stretched out into vagueness, but her telegrams revealed its magnitude.

Rose's cramped muscles stirred restlessly. There was barely room to move in the tiny office, crowded with table and chair and wastebasket. Spaciousness was on the other side of the counter.

She snatched the pencil from the counter and began a letter to Paul. Her imagination, at least, was released when she wrote letters.

Dear Paul:

I wonder what you are doing now! It's eight o'clock and of course you've had your supper. Your mother's probably finishing up the kitchen work and putting the bread to rise, and you haven't anything to do but sit on the porch and look at the stars and the lighted windows here and there in the darkness, and listen to the breeze in the trees. And here I am, sitting in a place that looks just like a hothouse with all the flowers come to life. There's a ball upstairs, and a million girls have gone through the corridors, with flowers and feathers and jewels in their hair, and dresses and evening cloaks as beautiful as petals. How I wish you could see them all, and the men, too, in evening dress. They're the funniest things when they're fat, but some of the slim ones look like princes or counts or something.

What kind of new furniture was it your mother got? You've never told me a word about the place you're living since you moved, and I'm awfully interested. Do please tell me what color the wallpaper is and the carpets, and the woodwork, and what the kitchen is like, and if there are rose bushes in the yard. Did your mother get new curtains, too? There is a lovely new material for curtains just out, sort of silky, and rough, in the loveliest colors. I see it in the store windows, and if your mother wants me to I'd love to price it, and get samples for her.

A little boy's just come in with a toy balloon, and it got away from him and it's bumping up around on the gilded ceiling, and I wish you could hear him howl. It must be fun for the balloon, though, after being dragged around for hours, tugging all the time to get away, to escape at last and go up and up and up.

I felt just like that this morning. Just think, Paul, I sent the last of the hundred dollars home, and another fifty besides! Isn't that gorgeous? I'm making over ninety dollars a month now, with my extra work at SF office, and my salary here

She paused, biting her pencil. That would give him a start, she thought. He had been so self-satisfied when he got his raise to being day-operator and station-agent. She had not quite got over the hurt of his taking it without letting her know that the night-operator's place would be vacant. He had explained that a girl couldn't handle the job, but she knew that he did not want her to be working with him.

In the spring, she thought, she would be able to get some beautiful new clothes and go home for a visit. Paul would come, too, when he knew she would be there. He would see then how well she could manage on a very little money. In a few months more she would be able to save enough for a trousseau, tablecloths, and embroidered towels . . .

"Blank, please!" A customer leaned on the counter. She gave him the pad and watched him while he wrote. His profile was handsome; a lock of fair hair beneath the pushed-back hat, a straight forehead, an aquiline nose, a thin, humorous mouth. He wrote rapidly, dashing the pencil across the paper, tearing off the sheet and crumpling it impatiently, beginning again. When he finished, shoving the message toward her with a quick movement, he looked at her and smiled, and she felt a charm in the warm flash of his eyes. His nervous vitality was magnetic.

Rose read the message. " 'C. G. Lane, Central Trust Company, Los Angeles. Drawing on you for five hundred. Must have it. Absolutely sure thing this time. Full explanations follow by letter. Gillette.' Sixty-seven cents, please," she said. She wished that she could think of something more to say; she would have liked to talk to him. There was about him an impression of something happening every instant. When, turning away, he paused momentarily, she looked at him quickly. But he was speaking to the rival operator.

"Hello, doll!"

"On your way," the girl replied imperturbably. Her eyes laughed and challenged. But with an answering smile he went past, and only his hat remained visible in glimpses through the crowd. Then it turned a corner and was gone.

"Fresh!" the girl murmured. "But gee, he can dance!"

Rose looked at her with interest. She was a new girl, on relief duty. The regular operator for Postal Telegraph was a sober, conscientious woman of thirty, who studied German grammar in her leisure moments. This one was not at all like her.

"Do you know him?" said Rose, smiling shyly. This was an opening for conversation, and she met it eagerly. The other girl had a friendly and engaging manner, which obviously included all the world.

"Sure I do," she answered, though there was uncertainty under the round tones. She ran a slim forefinger through the blond curl that lay against her neck, smiling at Rose with a display of even, white teeth. Rose thought of pictures on magazine covers. It must be wonderful to be as pretty as that, she thought wistfully. "Who's he wiring to?"

Rose passed the message across the low railing that separated the offices. She noticed the shining of the girl's fingernail as she ran it along the lines.

"Well, what do you know about that? He *wasn't* giving me a song and dance about being Judge Lane's son. You never can tell about men," she commented sagely, returning the telegram. "Sometimes they tell you the absolute truth."

A childlike quality made her sophistication merely piquant. Her comments on the passing guests fascinated Rose, and an occasional phrase revealed glimpses of a world of gaiety in which she seemed to flutter continually, like a butterfly in the sunshine. She worked, it appeared, only at irregular intervals.

"Momma supports me, of course, on her alimony. Papa certainly treated her rotten, but his money's perfectly good," she said artlessly. Her frankness also was childlike, and her calm acceptance of the situation made it necessary to regard it as commonplace. Rose, in self-defense, could not be shocked.

"She's a lot of fun, momma is. Just loves a good time. She's out dancing now. I wish I was! I'm just crazy about dancing, aren't you? Listen to that music! All I want is just to dance all night long. That's what I really love."

"Do you often do it? Dance all night long?" Rose asked, wide-eyed.

"Only once a night." She laughed. "About five nights a week."

Rose thought her entertaining, and warmed to her beauty and charm. In an hour she was asking Rose to call her Louise, and although she made no attempt to conceal her astonishment at the barrenness of Rose's life, her generous desire to share her own good times took the sting from her pity. Why, Rose didn't know the city at all, she cried, and Rose could only assent. They must go out to some of the cafes together; they must have tea at Techau's; Rose must come to dinner and meet momma. Louise jumbled a dozen plans together in a rush of friendliness. It was plain that she was genuinely touched in her butterfly heart by Rose's loneliness.

"And you're a brunette!" she cried. "We'll be stunning together. I'm so blonde." The small circle of her thought returned always to herself. Rose, dimly seeing this, felt an amused tolerance, which saved her pride while she confessed to herself her inferiority in cleverness to this sparkling small person. Louise would never have drifted into dull stagnation; she would have found some way to fill her life with realities instead of dreams.

Midnight came before Rose realized it. Tidying her desk for the night, she found the unfinished letter to Paul and tucked it into her purse. She had not been forced to feed upon her imagination that evening.

Louise walked to the car line with her, and it was settled that the next night Rose should come to dinner and meet momma. It meant cutting short her extra work and paying the day-operator to stay late at the St. Francis, but Rose did not regret the cost. This was the first friend the city had offered her.

Three weeks later she was sharing the apartment on Leavenworth Street with Louise and her momma.

The change had come with startling suddenness. There had been the dinner first. Rose approached it diffidently, doubtful of her self-possession in a strange place, with strange people. She fortified herself with a new hat and a veil with large velvet spots, yet at the very door she had a moment of panic and thought of flight and a telephone message of regrets. Only the thought of her desperate loneliness gave her courage to ring the bell.

The strain disappeared as soon as she met momma. Momma, slim in a silk petticoat and a frilly dressing-gown, had taken her in affectionately. Momma was much like Louise. Rose thought again of pictures on magazine covers, though Louise suggested a new magazine and her mother did not. Even Rose could see that momma's pearly complexion was liberally helped by powder, and her hair was almost unnaturally golden. But the eyes were the same, large and blue, fringed with black lashes, and both profiles had the same clear, delicate outlines.

"Yes, dear, most people do think we're sisters," Mrs. Latimer said complacently, when Rose spoke of the resemblance.

"We have awful good times together, don't we, Momma?" Louise added, her arm around her mother's waist, and Rose felt a pang at the fondness of the reply. "We certainly do, kiddo."

It was a careless, happy-go-lucky household. Dinner was scrambled together somehow, with much opening of cans, in a neglected, dingy kitchen. Rose and Louise washed the dishes while momma stirred the creamed chicken. It was fun to wash dishes again and to set the table, and Rose could imagine herself one of the family while she listened to their intimate chatter. They had had tea downtown; there was mention of someone's new car, somebody's diamonds; Louise had seen a lavalliere in a jeweler's shop; she teased her mother to buy it for her, and her mother said fondly, "Well, honey-baby, we'll see."

They had hardly begun to eat when the telephone rang, and momma, answering it, was gone for some time. They caught scraps of bantering talk and Louise wondered, "Who's that she's jollying now?" She sprang up with a cry of delight when momma came back to announce that the crowd was going to the beach.

There was a scramble to dress. Rose, hooking their gowns in the cluttered bedroom, saw dresser drawers overflowing with sheer underwear, silk stockings, bits of ribbon, and crushed hat trimmings. Louise brushed her eyebrows with a tiny brush, rubbed her nails with a buffer, dabbed carefully at her lips with lipstick. Rose hoped that she did not show her surprise at these novel details of the toilet.

They had taken it for granted she was going to the beach with them. Their surprise and regret were genuine when she said she must go to work.

"Oh, what do you want to do that for?" Louise pouted. "You look all right." She said it doubtfully, then brightened. "I'll lend you some of my things. You'd be perfectly stunning dressed up. You've got lovely hair and that baby stare of yours . . . All you need's a dress and a little make-up—don't you think, Momma?"

Her mother agreed warmly. Rose glowed under their praise and was deeply grateful for their interest in her. She wanted very much to go with them, and when she stood on the sidewalk watching them depart in a big red automobile, amidst a chorus of gay voices, she felt chilled and lonely.

They were wonderful to be so friendly to her, she thought, while she went soberly to work. She felt that she must in some way return their kindness, and after discarding a number of plans she decided to take them both to a matinee.

It was Louise, at their third meeting, who suggested that she come to live with them. "Do you know, Momma, Rose's living in some awful hole all alone. Why couldn't she come in with us? She could sleep in my room. Momma, why not?"

Her mother, smiling lazily, said:

"Well, if you kids want to, I don't care." Rose was delighted by the prospect. It was arranged that she should pay one third of the expenses, and Louise cried joyfully: "Now, Momma, you've got to get my lavalliere!"

The next afternoon Rose packed her bag and left the room on Gough Street. Her feet wanted to dance when she went down the narrow stairs for the last time and let herself out into the windy sunshine.

It was maddening to find herself so tied down by her work. In the early mornings, dragging herself from bed, she left Louise drowsy among the pillows and saw while she dressed the tantalizing signs of last night's gaiety in the dress flung over a chair, the scattered slippers and silk stockings. She came home at midnight to a dark, silent apartment, letting herself in with a latch-key to find the dinner dishes still unwashed and spatterings of powder on the bedroom carpet, where street shoes and a discarded petticoat were tangled together. She enjoyed putting things in order, pretending the place was her own while she did it, but she was lonely. Later she awoke to blink at Louise, sitting half undressed on the edge of the bed, rubbing her face with cold-cream, and to listen sleepily to her chatter.

"You'll be a long time dead, kiddo," momma said affectionately. "What's the use of being a dead one till you have to?" Rose's youth cried that momma was right. But she knew too well the miseries of being penniless; she dared not give up a job. A chance remark, flung out on the endless flow of Louise's gossip, offered the solution. "What do you know about that boob girl at the MX office? She's picked a chauffeur in a garden of millionaires, and she's going to quit work and *marry* him!"

Rose's heart leaped. It was her chance. When she confronted Mr. Bryant across the main office counter the next morning her hands trembled, but her whole nature had hardened into a cold determination. She would get that job. It paid sixty dollars a month; the hours were from eight to four. Whether she could handle market reports or not did not matter; she *would* handle them.

She scored her first business triumph when she got this job, although she did not realize until many years later what a triumph it had been. She settled into her work at the Merchants' Exchange wires with only one thought. Now she was free to live normally, to have a good time, like other girls.

The first day's work strained her nerves to the breaking point. The shouts of buyers and sellers on the floor, the impatient pounding on the counter of customers with rush messages, the whole breathless haste and excitement of the exchange, blurred into an indistinct clamor through which she heard only the slow, heavy working of the Chicago wire, tapping out a meaningless jumble of letters and fractions. She concentrated upon it, with an effort which made her a blind machine. The scrawled quotations she flung on the counter were wrought from an agony of nerves and brain.

But it was over at last, and Rose hurried home. The dim stillness of the apartment was an invitation to rest, but she disregarded it, slipping out of her shirtwaist and splashing her face and bare arms with cold water. A new chiffon blouse was waiting in its box, and a thrill of anticipation ran through her when she lifted it from its tissue wrappings.

She fastened the soft folds, pleased by the lines of her round arms seen through the transparency, and her slender neck rising from white frills. In the hand-glass she gazed at the oval of her face reflected in the dressing table mirror, and suddenly lifting her lids caught the surprising effect of the sea-gray eyes beneath black lashes, an effect she had never known until Louise spoke of it.

She was pretty. She was almost—she caught her breath—beautiful. The knowledge was more than beauty itself, for it brought self-assurance. She felt equal to any situation the evening might offer, and she was smiling at herself in the mirror when Louise burst in, a picture in a dashing white serge suit and a hat whose black line was like the stroke of an artist's pencil.

"The alimony's come!" she cried. "We're going to have a regular time! Momma'll meet us down town. Look, isn't it stunning?" She displayed the longed-for lavalliere twinkling against her smooth young neck. "I knew I'd get it somehow. Momma—the stingy thing!—she went and got her new furs. But we met Bob, and he bought it for me." She sat down before the mirror, throwing off her hat and letting down her hair. "I don't know; it's only a chip diamond." Her moods veered as swiftly as light summer breezes. "I wish momma'd get me a real one. It's nonsense, her treating me like a baby. I'm seventeen."

Rose felt her delight in the new waist evaporate. Louise's chatter always made her feel at a disadvantage. There was a distance between them that they seemed unable to bridge, and Rose realized that it was her fault. Perhaps it was because she had been so long alone that she often felt even more lonely when she was with Louise.

The sensation returned, overpowering, when they joined the crowd in the restaurant. She could only follow Louise's insouciant progress through a bewildering medley of voices, music, brilliant lights, and stumble into a chair at a table ringed with strange faces. Momma was there, her hat dripping with plumes, white furs flung negligently over her shoulders, her fingers a blaze of rings. There was another resplendent woman, named Nell Allan; a bald-headed fat man called Bob; a younger man with a lean face and restless blue eyes, hailed by Louise as Duddy. They were having a very gay time, but Rose, shrinking unnoticed in her chair, was unaccountably isolated and lonely. She could think of nothing to say. There was no thread in the rapid chatter at which she could clutch. They were all talking, and every phrase seemed a flash of wit, since they all laughed so much.

"I love the cows and chickens, but this is the life!" Duddy cried at intervals. "Oh, you chickens!" and "This is the life!" the others responded in a chorus of merriment. Rose did not doubt that it all meant something, but her wits were too slow to grasp it, and the talk raced on unintelligibly. She could only sit silent eating delicate food from plates that waiters whisked into place and whisked away again, and laughing uncertainly when the others did.

Color and light and music beat upon her brain. About her was a confusion of movement, laughter, clinking glasses, glimpses of white shoulders and red lips, perfumes, hurrying waiters, steaming dishes, and over and through it all the quick, accented rhythm of the music, swaying, dominating, blending all sensations into one quickening vibration.

Suddenly, from all sides, hidden in the artificial foliage that covered the walls, silvery bells took up the melody. Rose, inarticulate and motionless, felt her nerves tingle, alive, joyful, eager.

There was a pushing back of chairs, and she started. But they were only going to dance. Duddy and momma, Bob and Mrs. Allan, swept out into a whirl of white arms and dark coats, tilted faces and swaying bodies. "Isn't it lovely!" Rose murmured.

But Louise was not listening. She sat mutinous, her fingers tapping time to the music, her eyes beneath the long lashes searching the room. "I can't help it. I've just got to dance!" she muttered, and suddenly she was gone. Someone met her among the tables, put his arms around her, and whirled her away. Rose, watching for her black hat and happy face to reappear, saw that she was dancing with the man whose telegram had introduced them. Memory finally gave her his name. Gillette Lane.

Louise brought him to the table when the music ceased. There were gay introductions, and Rose wished that she could say something. But momma monopolized him, squeezing in an extra chair for him beside her, and saying how glad she was to meet a friend of her little girl's.

Rose could only be silent, listening to their incomprehensible gaiety, and feeling an attraction for him as irresistible as an electric current. She did not know what it was, but she thought him the handsomest man she had ever seen, and she felt that he did whatever he wanted to do with invariable success. He was not like the others. He talked their jargon, but he did not seem of them, and she noticed that his hazel eyes, set in a network of tiny wrinkles, were at once avid and weary. Yet he could not be older than twenty-eight or so. He danced with momma, when again the orchestra began a rag, but coming back to the table with the others, he said restlessly:

"Let's go somewhere else. My car's outside. How about the beach?"

"Grand little idea!" Duddy declared amid an approving chorus. Rose, following the others among the tables and through the swinging doors to the curb where the big gray car stood waiting, told herself that she must make an effort, must pay for this wonderful evening with some contribution to the fun. But when they had all crowded into the machine and she felt the rush of cool air against her face and saw the street lights speeding past, she forgot everything but joy. She was having a good time at last, and a picture of the Mansfield girls flashed briefly through her mind. How meager their picnics and hay rides appeared beside this!

She half formed the phrases in which she would describe to Paul their racing down the long boulevard beside the beach, the salty air, and the darkness, and the long white lines of foam upon the breakers. This, she realized with exultation, was a joy-ride. She had read the word in newspapers, but its aptness had never before struck her.

It was astounding to find, after a rush through the darkness, that the car was stopping. Everyone was getting out. Amazed and trying to conceal her amazement, she went with them through a blaze of light into another restaurant where another orchestra played the same gay music and dancers whirled beyond a film of cigarette smoke. They sat down at a round bare table, and Rose perceived that one must order something to drink.

She listened to the rapid orders, hesitating. "Blue moons" were intriguing, and "slow gin fizz" was fascinating with its suggestion of fireworks. But beside her Mr. Lane said, "Scotch highball," and the waiter took her hesitation for repetition. The glass appeared before her, there was a cry of "Happy days!" and she swallowed a queer-tasting, stinging mouthful. She set the glass down hastily.

"What's the matter with the highball?" Mr. Lane inquired. He had paid the waiter, and she felt the obligation of a guest.

"It's very good really. But I don't care much for drinks that are fizzy," she said. She saw a faint amusement in his eyes, but he did not smile, and his order to the waiter was peremptory. "Plain highball here, no seltzer." The waiter hastened to bring it.

Mr. Lane's attention was still upon her, and she saw no escape. She smiled at him over the glass. "Happy days!" she said and drank. She set down the empty glass and the muscles of her throat choked back a cough. "Thank you," she said, and was surprised to find that the weariness was no longer in his eyes.

"You're all right!" he said. His tone was that of the vanquished greeting the victor, and his next words were equally enigmatic. "I hate a bluffer that doesn't make good when he's called!" The orchestra had swung into a new tune, and he half rose. "Dance?"

It was hard to admit her deficiency and let him go.

"I can't. I don't know how."

He sat down.

"You don't know how to dance?" His inflection said that this was carrying pretense too far, that in overshooting a mark she had missed it. His keen look at her suddenly made clear a fact for which she had been unconsciously groping while she watched these men and women, the clue to their relations. Beneath their gaiety a ceaseless game was being played, man against woman, and every word and glance was a move in that game, the basis of which was enmity. He thought that she, too, was playing it, and against him.

"Why do you think I'm lying to you, Mr. Lane? I would like to dance if I could, of course."

"I don't get you," he replied with equal directness. "What do you come out here for if you don't drink and don't dance?"

It would be too humiliating to confess the extent of her inexperience, her ignorance of the city in which she had lived for almost a year. "I come because I like it," she said. "I've worked hard for a long time and never had any fun. And I'm going to learn to dance. I don't know about drinking. I don't like the taste of it much. Do people really like to drink highballs and things like that?"

It startled a laugh from him.

"Keeping on drinking 'em, and you'll find out why people do it," he answered. Over his shoulder he said to the waiter, "A couple more Scotch highballs, Ben."

The others were dancing. They were alone at the table, and when, resting an elbow on the edge of it, he concentrated his attention upon her, the crowded room became a swirl of color and light about their isolation.

Rose's breath came faster, the toe of her slipper kept time to the music, exhilaration mounted in her veins, and her success in holding his interest was like wine to her. But a cold, keen inner self took charge of her brain.

The highballs arrived. She did not drink hers, and thought that she was rude. When he urged she refused as politely as she could. He insisted.

"Drink it!" She felt the clash of an imperious reckless will against her impassive resistance. There was a second in which neither moved, and their whole relation subtly changed. Then she laughed.

"I'd really rather not," she said lightly.

"Come on, be game," he said.

"The season's closed." Louise's flippancies had not been without their effect on Rose. It was easier to drop back into her own language. "Tell me, why do people drink things that taste like that?"

He met her on her own ground. "You've got to drink, to let go, to have a good time. It breaks down inhibitions." She noted the word. The use of such words was one of the things that marked his difference from the others. "God knows why," he added wearily. "But what's the use of living if you don't hit the high spots? And there's a streak of depravity in me that's got to have this kind of thing."

Their group swooped down about the table, and the general ordering of more drinks ended their talk. There was a clamor when Rose said she did not want anything. Duddy swept away her protests and ordered for her, but momma came to the rescue.

"Let the kid alone; she's not used to it. You stick to lemon sours, baby. Don't let them kid you," she said. The chatter swept on, leaving her once more unnoticed, but when the music called again Mr. Lane took her out among the dancers.

"You're all right," he said. "Just let yourself go and

follow me. It's only a walk to music." And unaccountably she found herself dancing, felt the rhythm beat through blood and nerves, and stiffness and awkwardness drop away from her. She felt like a butterfly bursting from a chrysalis, like a bird singing in the dawn. She was so happy that Mr. Lane laughed at the ecstasy in her face.

"You look like a kid in a candy-shop," he said, swinging her past a jam with a long-breathless swooping glide and picking up the step again.

"I'm per-fect-ly happy!" she cried, in time to the tune. "It's aw-ful-ly good of you-ou!"

He laughed again.

"Stick with me and I'll teach you a lot of things," he said.

She found, when she went reluctantly back to the table with him, that the others were talking of leaving. It hurt to hear him enthusiastically greeting the suggestion. But after they were in the car it appeared that they were not going home. There was an interval of rushing through the cool darkness, and then another restaurant just like the others, and more dancing.

The hours blurred into a succession of those swift dashes through the clean night air, and recurring plunges into light and heat and smoke and music. Rose, faithfully sticking to lemon sours as momma had advised, discovered that she could dance something called a rag, and something else known as a Grizzly Bear, heard Duddy crying that she was some chicken, and felt herself a great success. Bob was growing strangely sentimental and talked sorrowfully about his poor old mother; momma's cheeks were flushed under the rouge, and she sang part of a song, forgetting the rest of the words. The crowd shifted and separated; somewhere they lost part of it, and a stranger appeared with Louise.

Rose, forced at last to think of her work next morning,

was horrified to find that it was two o'clock. Momma agreed that the best of friends must part. They sang while they sped through the sleeping city, the stars overhead and the street lights flashing by. Drowsily happy, Rose thought it no harm to rest her head on Mr. Lane's shoulder, and she wondered what it would be like if a man so fascinating were in love with her. It would be frightfully thrilling and exciting, she thought, playing daringly with the idea.

"See you later!" they all cried, when she alighted with momma and Louise before the dark apartment house. The others were going on to more fun somewhere. She shook hands with Mr. Lane, feeling a contraction of her heart. "Thank you for a very pleasant time." She felt that he was amused by the stilted words.

"Don't forget it isn't the last one!" he said.

Rose did not forget. The words repeated themselves in her mind; she heard his voice, and felt his arm around her waist and the music throbbing in her blood for a long time. The sensations came back to her in the pauses of her work next day, while she dragged through the hours as if she were drugged, hearing the noise of the exchange and market quotations clicking off the Chicago wire, now very far and thin, now close and sickeningly loud.

She was white and felt limp when she got home, and momma suggested a bromo-seltzer and offered to lend her some rouge. But Mr. Lane had not telephoned, and she went to bed instead of going out with them that evening. It was eleven days before he did telephone.

Chapter 9

In the mornings Rose went to work. The first confusion of the Merchants' Exchange had cleared a little. She began to see a pattern in the fluctuations of the market quotations. January wheat, March rye, May corn, became a drama to her, and while she snatched the figures from the wire and tossed them to the waiting boy, saw them chalked up on the huge board, and heard the shouts of the brokers, she caught glimpses of the world-wide gamble in lives and fortunes.

But it was only another great spectacle in which she had no part. She was merely a living mechanical attachment to the network of wires. She wanted to tear herself away, to have a life of her own, a life that went forward, instead of swinging like a pendulum between home and the office.

Rose did not want to work. She had never wanted to work. Working had been only a means of reaching sooner her own life with Paul. The road had run straight before her to that end. But now Paul would not let her follow it; he did not want her to work with him at Ripley; she would have to wait until he made money enough to support her. And she hated work.

Resting her chin on one palm, listening half consciously for her call to interrupt the ceaseless clicking of the sounder, she gazed across the marble counter and the vaulted room; the gesticulating brokers, the scurrying messengers, faded into a background against which she saw again the light and color and movement of the night when she had met Mr. Lane. She heard his voice. "What's the use of living if you don't hit the high spots?"

She hurried home at night, expecting she knew not what. But it had not happened. Restlessness took possession of her, and she turned for hours on her pillow, dozing only to hear the clicking of telegraph-sounders, and music, and to find herself dancing on the floor of the Merchants' Exchange with a strange man who had Mr. Lane's eyes. On the eleventh day she received a letter from Paul which quieted the turmoil of her thoughts like a dash of cold water. In his even neat handwriting he wrote:

> I suppose the folks you write about are all right. They sound pretty queer to me. I don't pretend to know anything about San Francisco, though. But I don't see how you are going to hold down a job and keep up with the way they seem to spend their time, though I will not say anything about dancing. You know I could not do it and stay in the church, but I do not mean to bring that up again in a letter. You were mighty fine and straight and sincere about that, and if you do not feel the call to join I would not urge you. But I do not think I would like your new friends. I would rather a girl was not so pretty, but used less slang when she talks.

The words gained force by echoing a stifled opinion of her own. With no other standard than her own instinct, she had had moments of criticizing Louise and momma. But she had quickly hidden the criticism in the depth of her mind, because they were companions and she had not been able to find any others. Now they stood revealed through Paul's eyes as glaringly cheap and vulgar.

Her longing for a good time, if she must have it with such people, appeared weak and foolish to her. She felt older and steadier when she went home that night. Then, just as she entered the door, the telephone rang and Louise called that Gillette Lane wanted to speak to her.

It was impossible to analyze his fascination. Uncounted times she had gone over all he had said, all she could conjecture about him, vainly seeking an explanation of it. The mere sound of his voice revived the spell like an incantation, and her half-hearted resistance succumbed to it.

Before the dressing-table, hurrying to make herself beautiful for an evening with him, Rose leaned closer to the glass and tried to find the answer in the gray eyes looking back at her. But they only grew eager, and her reflection faded, to leave her brooding on the memory of his face, half mocking and half serious, and the tired hunger of his eyes.

"Have a heart, for the lova Mike!" cried Louise. "Give me a chance. You aren't using the mirror yourself, even!" She slipped into the chair Rose left and, pushing back her mass of golden hair, gazed searchingly at her face. "Got to get my lashes dyed again; they're growing out. Say, you certainly did make a hit with Lane!"

"Where's the nail polish?" Rose asked, searching in the hopeless disorder of the bureau drawers. "Oh, here it is. What do you know about him?"

"Well, he's one of those Los Angeles Lanes. His father was indicted for something awhile ago. Loads of money." Louise, dabbing on cold-cream, spoke in jerks.

Momma, slipping a rustling gown over her head, spoke through the folds. "He's a live wire," she praised. She settled the straps over her shoulders, tossing a fond smile at

Rose. "Hook me up, dearie? Yes, he's a live wire all right, and you've certainly got him coming."

A sudden thought chilled Rose to the fingertips. She fumbled with the hooks.

"He isn't married, is he?"

"Married! Well, I should say not! What do you think I am?" momma demanded. "Do you think I'd steer you or Louise up against anything like that?" Her voice softened. "I know too well what unhappiness comes from someone taking another lady's husband away from his home and family, though he does pay the alimony regular as the day comes around, I will say that for him. I hope never to live to see the day my girl, or you either, does a thing like that." There was genuine emotion in her voice. Rose felt a rush of affectionate pity for her, and Louise, springing up, threw her bare arms around her mother.

"Don't you worry, angel Momma! Never!" she cried.

At such moments of warm-hearted sincerity Rose was fond of them both. She felt ashamed while she finished dressing. They were lovely to her, she thought, and they accepted people as they were, without sneaking little criticisms and feelings of superiority. She did not know what she thought about anything.

Her indecisions were cut short by the squawk of an automobile horn beneath the windows. With last hasty slaps of powderpuffs and a snatching of gloves, they hurried down to meet Mr. Lane at the door, and again Rose felt his charm like a tangible current between them. Words choked in her throat, and she stood silent in a little whirlpool of greetings.

There were three indistinct figures already in the tonneau; a glowing cigar-end lighted a fat, jolly face, and two feminine voices greeted momma and Louise. Hesitating on the curb, Rose felt a warm, possessive hand close on her arm.

"Get out, Dick. Climb in back. This little girl's going in front with me." The dominating voice made the words like an irresistible force. Not until she was sitting beside him and a docile young man had wedged himself into the crowded space behind, did it occur to her to question it.

"Do you always boss people like that?"

They were racing smoothly down a slope, and his answer came through the rushing of the wind past her ears. "Always." The gleam of a headlight passed across his face and she saw it keen, alert, intensely alive. "Ask, and you'll have to argue. Command, and people jump. It's the man that orders what he wants that gets it. Philosophy taught in ten lessons," he added in a contemptuous undertone. "Well, little girl, you haven't been forgetting me, have you?"

She disregarded the change of tone. His idea had struck her as extraordinarily true. It had never occurred to her. She turned it over in her mind.

"A girl ought to be able to work it, too," she said.

He laughed.

"Maybe. She finds it easier to work a man."

"I'm too polite to agree that all of you are soft things."

"You're too clever to find any of us hard to handle."

"Yes? Isn't it too bad putty is so uninteresting?"

She was astounded at her own words. They came from her lips with no volition of her own, leaping automatically in response to his. She felt only the stimulation of his interest, of his electrical presence beside her, of their swift rush through the darkness pierced by flashing lights.

"You don't, of course, compare me to putty?"

"Well, of course, it does set and stay put, in the end. You can depend on it."

"You can count on me, all right. I'm crazy about you."

"Crazy people are unaccountable."

Her heart was racing. The speed of the car, the rush of

the air, were in her veins. She had never dreamed that she could talk like this. This man aroused in her qualities she had never known she possessed, and their discovery intoxicated her.

He was silent a moment, turning the car into a quieter street. There was laughter behind them; one of the others called: "We should worry about the cops! Go to it, Gil!" He did not reply, and the leap of the car swept their chatter backward again.

"Going too fast for you?" She read a double meaning and a challenge in the words.

"I've never gone too fast!" she answered. "I love to ride like this. Where are we going?"

"Anywhere you want to go, as long as it's with me."

"Then let's just keep going and never get there. Do you know what I thought you meant the other night when you said we'd go to the beach?"

"No, what?" He was interested.

She told him. This was safer ground, and she enlarged her mental picture of the still, moonlit beach, the white breakers foaming along the shore, the salt wind, and the darkness, and the car plunging down a long white boulevard.

"Do you mean to tell me you'd never been to the beach resorts before?"

"Isn't it funny?" she laughed.

"You're a damn game little kid."

She found that the words pleased her more than anything he had yet said.

They sped on in silence. Rose found occupation enough in the sheer delight of going so swiftly through a blur of light and darkness toward an unknown end. She did not resist the fascination of the man beside her; there was exhilaration in his being there, security in his necessary attention to handling the automobile. They passed the park gates, and the car leaped like a live thing at the touch of a whip, plunging faster down the smooth road between dark masses of shrubbery. A clean, moist odor of the forest mixed with a salt tang in the air, and the headlights were like funnels of light cutting into the solid night a space for them to pass.

"Isn't it wonderful!" Rose sighed, and despised the inadequacy of the word.

"I like the bright lights better myself." After a pause, he added, "Country bred, aren't you?"

She replied in the same tone.

"College man, I suppose."

"How did you dope that?"

" 'Inhibitions,' " she answered.

"What? O-o-oh! So you haven't been forgetting me?"

"I didn't forget the word," she said. "I looked it up."

"Well, make up your mind to get rid of 'em?"

"I'd get rid of anything I didn't want."

"Going to get rid of me?"

"No," she said coolly. "I'll just let you go."

It struck her that she was utterly mad. She had never dreamed of talking like that to anyone. What was she doing and why?

"Don't you believe it one minute!" His voice had the dominating ring again, and suddenly she felt that she had started a force she was powerless to control. The situation was out of her hands, running away with her. Her only safety was silence, and she shrank into it.

When the car stopped she jumped out of it quickly and attached herself to momma. In the hot, smoky room they found a table at the edge of the dancing floor, and she slipped into the chair farthest from him, ordering lemonade. Exhilaration left her; again she could think of nothing that seemed worth saying, and she felt his amused eyes upon her while she sat looking at the red crepe paper decorations overhead and the maze of dancing couples. It was some time before the rhythm of the music began to beat in her blood and the scene lost its tawdriness and became gay.

"Everybody's doing it now!" Louise hummed, looking at him under her long lashes. The others were dancing, and the three sat alone at the table. "Everybody's doing it, doing it, doing it. Everbody's doing it, but you, and me."

"Go and grab off somebody else," he answered good-humoredly. "I'm dancing with Rose, when she gets over being afraid of me." He lighted a cigarette casually.

"Oh, really? I'd love to dance. Only I don't do it very well."

His arms were around her and they were dancing before she perceived how neatly she had risen to the bait. She stumbled and lost a step in her fury.

"No? Not afraid of me?" he laughed. "Well, don't be. What's the use?"

"It isn't that," she said. "Only I don't know how to play your game. And I don't want to play it. And I'm not going to. You're too clever."

"Don't be afraid," he said, and his arm tightened. They missed step again, and she lost the swing of the music. "Let yourself go, relax," he ordered. "Let the music—that's better."

They circled the floor again, but her feet were heavy, and the knowledge that she was dancing badly added to her effort. Phrases half formed themselves in her mind and escaped. She wanted to be able to carry off the situation well, to make her meaning clear in some graceful, indirect way, but she could not.

"It's this way," she said. "I'm not your kind. Maybe I talked that way for a while, but I'm not really. I wish you'd leave me alone. I really do."

The music ended with a crash, and two thumps of many

feet echoed the last two notes. He still held her close, and she felt that inexplicable charm like the attraction of a magnet for steel.

"You really do?" His tone thrilled her with an intoxicating warmth. The smile in his eyes was both caressing and confident. Consciously she kept back the answering smile it commanded, looking at him gravely.

"I really do."

"All right." His quick acquiescence was exactly what she had wanted, and it made her unhappy. They walked back to the table, and for hours she was very gay, watching him dance with momma and Louise. She crowded into the tonneau during their quick, restless dashes from one dancing place to the next. She laughed a great deal, and when they met Duddy and Bob somewhere a little after midnight she danced with each of them. But she felt that having a good time was almost as hard work as earning a living.

It was nearly two weeks before she went out again with momma and Louise, and this time she did not see him at all. Louise was astonished by his failure to telephone.

"What in the world did you do with that Lane man?" she wanted to know. "You must have been an awful boob. Why, he was simply dippy about you. Believe me, I'd have strung him along if I'd had your chance. And an automobile like a palace car, too!" she mourned.

"Oh, well, baby, Rose doesn't know much about handling men," momma comforted her. "She did the best she could. You never can tell about 'em, anyway. And maybe he's out of town."

But this was not true, for Louise had seen him only that afternoon with a stunning girl in a million dollars' worth of sables.

Rose was swept by cross-currents of feeling. She told herself that she did not care what he did. She repeated this until she saw that the repetition proved its untruth. Then she let her imagination follow him. But it could do this only blindly. She could picture his home only by combining the magnificence of the St. Francis with scraps from novels she had read, and while she could see him running up imposing steps, passing through a great door and handing his coat to a dignified man servant, either a butler or a footman, she could not follow him further. She could see him with a beautiful girl at a table in a private room of a cafe; there were no longer any veils between her and that side of a man's life, and she no longer shrank from facing the world as it exists. But she knew that this was only one of his many interests and occupations. She would have liked to know the others.

She turned to thoughts of Paul as one comes from a dark room into clear light. At times she felt an affection for him that made her present life seem like a feverish dream. She imagined herself living in a pretty little house with him. There would be white curtains at the windows and roses over the porch. When the housework was all beautifully done she would sit on the porch, embroidering a centerpiece or a dainty waist. The gate would click, and he would come up the walk, his feet making a crunching sound on the gravel. She would run to meet him. It had been so long since she had seen him that his face was vague. When with an effort she brought from her memory the straight-looking blue eyes, the full, firm lips, the cleft in his chin, she saw how boyish he looked. He was a dear boy.

The days went by, each like the day before. The rains had begun. Every morning, in a ceaseless drizzle from gray skies, Rose rushed down a sidewalk filmed with running water and crowded into a streetcar jammed with irritated people and dripping umbrellas. When she reached the office her feet were wet and cold and the hems of her skirts flapped damply at her ankles.

She had a series of colds, and her head ached while she copied endless quotations from relentlessly clicking sounders. At night she rode wearily home, clinging to a strap, and crawled into bed. Her muscles ached and her throat was sore. Momma, even in the scurry of dressing from the evening, stopped to bring her a glass of hot whiskey-and-water, and she drank it gratefully. When at last she was alone she read awhile before going to sleep. One forgot the dreariness of living, swept away into an artificial world of adventure and romance.

Christmas came, and she recklessly spent money for gifts to send home: socks and ties and a shaving cup for her father, a length of black silk and a ten-dollar gold piece for her mother. They made an exciting bundle, and when she stood in line at the post office she pictured happily the delight there would be when it was opened. She hated work with a hatred that increased daily, but there was a deep satisfaction in feeling that she could do such things as this with money she herself had earned.

The brokers at the Merchants' Exchange gave her twenty dollars at Christmas, and with this she bought a gilt vanity-case for Louise, gloves for momma, and Paul's present. She thought a long time about that and at last chose a monogrammed stick-pin, with an old English "P" deeply cut in the gold.

He sent her a celluloid box lined with puffed pink sateen, holding a comb and brush set. It made a poor showing among the flood of presents that poured in for momma and Louise, but she would have been ashamed of being ashamed of it. However, she let them think it came from her mother. She had not told them about Paul, feeling a dim necessity of shielding that part of her life from Louise's comments.

There were parties every night Christmas week, but she did not go to any of them. She was in the throes of grippe, and though the work at the office was light it took all of her energy. Even on New Year's night she stayed at home, resisting all the urgings of Louise and momma, who told her she was missing the time of her life. She went resolutely to bed, to lie in the darkness and realize that it was New Year's night, that her life was going by and she was getting nothing she wanted. "It's the man that orders what he wants that gets it." Gillette Lane's voice came back to her.

Rain was beating on the window-panes, and through the sound of it she heard the distant uproar of many voices and a constant staccato of fireworks crackling through the dripping night in triumphant expression of the inextinguishable gaiety of the city. She thought of Paul. So much had happened since she saw him, so much had come between them. He had been living and growing older, too. It was impossible to see what his real life had been through his matter-of-fact letters, chronicles of where he had been, how much money he was saving, on which Sundays the minister had had dinner at his house. Only occasional phrases were clear in her memory. "When we are married—" She could still thrill over that. And he always signed his letters, "lovingly, Paul." And once, speaking of a Sunday-school picnic, he had written, "I wish you had been there. There was no girl that could touch you."

But Paul never mentioned when they might be married. How long was it going to be? Would she go on working forever, and never get anything she wanted? She saw weeks and months and years of work stretching ahead of her like the interminable series of ties in a railroad track, vanishing in as barren a perspective.

For nearly three years her whole life had been work. Those few evenings at the cafes had been her only gaiety. She had copied innumerable market quotations, sent uncounted messages, been a mere machine, and for what? She did not want to work, she wanted to live.

That night she went to the beach with the crowd. Bob

was there and Duddy and a score of others she had met in cafes. There again was the stir of shifting colors under brilliant lights, the eddy and swirl of dancers, sparkling eyes, white hands, a glimmer of rings, perfume, laughter, and through it all the music, throbbing, swaying, blending all sensations into one quickening rhythm, one exhilarating vibration of nerves and spirit. Rose felt weariness slip from her shoulders; she felt that she was soaring like a lark; she could have burst into song.

She danced. She danced eagerly, joyously, carried by the music as by the crest of a wave. Repartee slipped from her lips as readily as from Louise's; she found that it did not matter what one said, only that one said it quickly; her sallies were met by applauding laughter. In the automobile, dashing from place to place, she took off her hat and, facing the rushing wind, sang aloud for pure joy.

They encountered Gillette Lane just after midnight. She turned a flushed, radiant face to him when he came over to their table. She felt sure of herself; ready for anything. He leaned past her to shake hands with momma, who greeted him in chorus with Louise.

"Back in our midst once more!" he said to Rose over his shoulder. He brought up a chair beside hers, and she saw in his first glance that he was tired and moody. He ordered straight Scotch and snapped his fingers impatiently until the waiter brought it.

"Who you with, Gil? Didn't see your car outside," said Duddy.

"Oh, I was with some crowd. Don't know where they are. Haven't got the car," he answered.

"Stick around with us then." "I bet you've been hitting the high spots, and smashed it!" Bob and Duddy said simultaneously. But the orchestra was beginning another tune, and only Rose noticed that in the general pushing back of chairs he did not reply.

She shook her head at the question in his eyes, and he

asked no one else to dance. Of course, after that, she had to refuse the others, too, and they were left sitting at the bare table ringed with the imprints of wet glasses. An unaccountable depression was settling on her; she felt sorry and full of pity, she did not know why, and an impulse to put her hand on his smooth, fair hair surprised and horrified her.

"Rotten life, isn't it?" he said. It was a tone so new in him that she did not know how to reply.

"I'm sorry," she answered.

"Sorry? Good Lord, what for?"

"I don't know. I just am. I'm sorry for whatever it is that's happened." She saw that she had made a mistake, and the remnant of her exhilaration fluttered out like a spent candle. She sat looking at the dancers in silence, and they appeared to her peculiar and curious, going round and round with terrific energy, getting nowhere. The music had become an external thing, too, and she observed the perspiring musicians working wearily, with glances at the clock.

"Funny," she said at length.

"What?"

"All these people—and me, too—doing this kind of thing. We don't get anything out of it. What do we do it for?"

"Oh, safety-valve. Watts discovered the steam engine on the principle." His voice was very tired.

The more she considered the idea, the more her admiration for him grew. She was not in the least afraid of him now; she was eager to talk to him. Her hand went out detainingly when he rose, but he disregarded it. "So long," he said carelessly, and she saw that, absorbed in some preoccupation, he hardly knew that she was there. She let him go and sat turning an empty glass between her fingers, lost in speculations concerning him. Though she spent many of her evenings at the beach during several weeks, she did not see him again, and she heard one night that he had gone broke and left town.

She could not believe that disaster had conquered him. That last meeting and his disappearance had increased the charm he had for her. Her mind returned frequently to him, drawn by an irresistible fascination. She had only to brood on the memory of him for a moment and a thrill ran through her body. It could not be that she loved him. Why, she did not even know him.

And to her mother she wrote:

As far as spending my time in making the right sort of acquaintance, I DO mean it in a "climbing way." It's easy enough to know the right sort of people and there's every advantage in the world in knowing 'em— if anyone means to climb at all she might as well climb all the time, and if she meets people at all, meet the right sort. Huh?

Chapter 10

In March Paul came to see her.

It had been a hard day at the office. A mistake had been made in a message, and a furious broker, asserting that it had cost him thousands of dollars, that she was at fault, that he was going to sue the telegraph company, had pounded the counter and refused to be quieted. All day Rose was overwhelmed with a sense of disaster. It would be months before the error was traced, and alternately she recalled distinctly that she had sent the right word and remembered with equal distinctness that she had sent the wrong one.

Dots and dashes jumbled together in her mind. She was exhausted at four o'clock, and thought eagerly of a hot bath and the soothing softness of a pillow. Slumped in the corner of the cablecar she endured its jerks and jolts, keeping a grip on herself with a kind of inner tenseness until the moment when she could relax.

Louise was hanging over the banister on the upper landing when she entered the hall of the apartment house. Her excited stage whisper met Rose on the stairs.

"Somebody's here to see you."

"Who?" The event was unusual, but Louise's manner was even more so. Vague pictures of her family and accident and death flashed through Rose's startled mind.

He said his name was Masters. He was an awful stick.
Momma'd sent Louise out to give her the high sign.
Louise's American Beauty salesman was in town and there
was going to be a party at the Cliff House. They could
sneak in and dress and beat it out the back way. Momma
had the guy in the living room. He'd simply spoil the
party.

"Momma'll get rid of him somehow. You can fix it up
afterward."

Rose's first thought was that Paul must not see her
looking like this, disheveled, her hair untidy, and her
fingers inkstained. Her heart was beating fast, and there
was a fluttering in her wrists. It was incredible that he was
really near, separated from her only by a partition. The
picture of him sitting there a victim of momma's efforts to
entertain him was ghastly and at the same time hysterically
comic. She tiptoed in breathless haste past the closed door
and gained the safety of the bedroom, Louise's kimono
rustling behind her. The first glance into the mirror was
sickening. She tore off her hat and coat and let down her
hair with trembling fingers.

"He's a very good friend. I must see him. Heavens! What
a fright! Be an angel and find me a clean waist?" Rose
whispered. The comb shook in her hand; hairpins slipped
through her fingers; the waist she found lacked a button,
and every pin in the room had disappeared. It was an
eternity before she was ready, and then, leaning for one last
look in the glass, she was dissatisfied. There was no color in
her face; even her lips were only palely pink. She bit them
till they reddened; then with a hurried resolve she scrubbed
her cheeks with Louise's rouge pad. That was better.
Another touch of powder!

"Do I look all right?"

"Stunning! Aw, Rose, who is he? You've never told me a
word." Louise was wild with curiosity.

"Later." Rose said. She drew a deep breath at the living-room door. Her little-girl shyness had come back upon her. Then she opened the door and walked in.

Momma, in her kimono, was sitting in the darkest corner of the room, with her back toward the window. Only a beaded slipper toe and some inches of silk stocking caught the light. She was obviously making conversation with painful effort. Paul sat facing her, erect in a stiff chair, his eyes fixed politely on a point over her shoulder. He rose with evident relief to meet Rose.

"Good afternoon, Mr. Masters," she said, embarrassed.

"Good afternoon." They shook hands.

"I'm very glad to see you. Won't you sit down?" she heard herself saying inanely.

Momma rose, clutching her kimono around her.

"Well, I'll be going, as I have a very important engagement, and you'll excuse me, Mr. Masters, I'm sure," she said archly. "So charmed to have met you," she added with artificial sweetness.

The closing of the door behind her left them facing each other with nothing but awkwardness between them. Paul had changed indefinably, though the square lines of his face, the honest blue eyes, the firm lips were as she remembered them. Under the smooth-shaven skin of his cheeks there was the blue shadow of a stubborn beard. He appeared prosperous, but not quite sure of himself, in a well-made broadcloth suit, and he held a new black derby hat in his left hand.

"I'm awfully glad to see you," Rose managed to say. "I'm so surprised! I didn't know you were coming."

"I sent you a telegram," he replied. "I wasn't sure until last night that I would come."

"I didn't get it," she said. Silence hung over them like a threat. "I'm sorry I didn't know. I hope you didn't have to wait long. I'm glad you're looking so well. How is your mother?"

"She's all right. How is yours?"

"She's very well, thank you." She caught her laugh on a hysterical note. "Well, how do you like San Francisco weather?"

His bewilderment faded slowly into a grin.

"It is rather hard to get started," he admitted. "You look different than I thought you would, somehow. But I guess we haven't changed much really. Can't we go somewhere else?"

She read his dislike of momma in the look he cast at her living-room. It was natural, no doubt. But a quick impulse of loyalty to these people who had been so kind to her illogically resisted it. This room with its close air, its film of dust over the table tops, its general air of neglect emphasized by the open candy box on the piano stool and the sooty papers in the gas grate, was nevertheless much pleasanter than the place where she had been living when she met Louise.

"I don't know just where," she replied. "Of course, I don't know the city very well because I work all day. But we might take a walk."

There was a scurry in the hallway when she opened the door; she caught a glimpse of Louise in petticoat and corset-cover dashing from the bathroom to the bedroom. Rose cast about quickly for something to say.

No, he answered, he could not stay in town long, only twenty-four hours. He wanted to see the superintendent personally about the proposition of putting in a spur-track at Ripley for the loading of melons. There were—her thoughts did not follow his figures. She heard vaguely something about irrigation districts and water-feet and sandy loam soil. So he had not come to see her!

Then Rose saw that he, too, was talking only to cover a sense of strangeness and embarrassment as sickening as her own. She wished that they were comfortably sitting down somewhere where they could talk. It was hard to say anything interesting while they walked along bleak streets with the wind snatching at them.

"Whew! You certainly have some wind in this town!" he exclaimed. At the top of Nob Hill its full force struck them, whipping her skirts and tugging at her hat while she stood gazing down at the gray honeycomb of the city and across it at masses of sea fog rolling over Twin Peaks. "It gives me an appetite, I'll tell you! Where'll we go for supper?"

Rose hesitated. She could not imagine his being comfortable in any of the places she knew. Music and brilliant lights and cabaret singers would be another barrier between them added to those she longed to break down. She said that she did not know the restaurants very well, and his surprise reminded her that she had written him pages about them. She stammered over an explanation she could not make.

There were so many small, unimportant things that were important because they could not be explained, and that could not be explained without making them more important than they were. It seemed to her that the months since they had last met were full of them.

She took refuge in talking about her work. But she saw that he did not like that subject. He said briefly that it was a rotten shame she had to do it, and obviously hoped to close the theme with that remark.

They found a small restaurant downtown, and after he had hung up his hat and they had discussed the menu, she sat turning a fork over and over and wondering what they could talk about. She managed to find something to say, but it seemed to her that their conversation had no more flavor than sawdust, and she was very unhappy.

"Look here, Rose, why didn't you tell those folks where you live that we're engaged?" There was nothing but inquiry in his tone, but the words were a bombshell. She straightened in her chair.

"Why—" How could she explain that vague feeling about keeping it from Louise and momma? "Why, I don't know. What was the use?"

"What was the use? Well, for one thing, it might have cleared things up a little for some of these other fellows that know you."

What had momma told him? "I don't know any men that would be interested," she said.

"Well, you never can tell about that," he answered reasonably. "I was sort of surprised, that's all. I had an idea girls talked over such things."

She was tired, and in the dull little restaurant there was nothing to stimulate her. The commonplace atmosphere, the warmth, and the placidity of his voice lulled her to stupidity.

"I suppose they do," she said. "They usually talk over their rings." She was alert instantly, filled with rage at herself and horror. His cheeks grew dully red. "I didn't mean—" she cried, and the words clashed with his. "If that's it I'll get you a ring."

"Oh, no! No! I don't want you to. I wouldn't think of taking it."

"Of course you know I haven't had money enough to get you a good one. I thought about it pretty often, but I didn't know you thought it was so important. Seems to me you've changed an awful lot since I knew you."

The protest, the explanation, was stopped on her lips. It was true. She felt that they had both changed so much that they might be strangers.

"Do you really think so?" she asked miserably.

"I don't know what to think," he answered honestly, pain in his voice. "I've been about crazy sometimes, thinking about things, wanting to see you again. And now, I don't know, you seem so different, sitting there with paint on your face" her hand went to her cheek as if it stung her "and talking about rings. You didn't use to be like this a bit, Rose," he went on earnestly. "It seems to me as if you'd completely lost track of your better self somehow. I wish you'd . . ."

This struck from her a spark of anger.

"Please don't begin preaching at me! I'm perfectly able to take care of myself. Really, Paul, you just don't understand. It isn't anything, really, a little bit of rouge. I only put it on because I was tired and didn't have any color. And I didn't mean it about the ring. I just didn't think what I was saying. But I guess you're right. I guess neither of us knows the other any more."

She felt desolate, abandoned to dreariness. Everything seemed all wrong with the world. She listened to Paul's assurances that he knew she was all right, whatever she did, that he didn't care anyhow, that she suited him. But they sounded hollow in her ears, for she knew that beneath them was the same uncertainty she felt. When, flushing, he said again that he would get her a ring, she answered that she did not want one, and they said no more about it. The abyss between them was left bridged only by the things they had not said, fearing to make it forever impassable by saying them.

He left her at her door promptly at the proper hour of ten. There was a moment in which a blind feeling in her reached out to him; she felt that they had taken hold of the situation by the wrong end somehow, that everything would be all right if they had had a chance.

He supposed she couldn't take the morning off. He had to see the superintendent, but maybe they could manage an hour or two. No, she had to work. With the threat of that missent message hanging over her she dared not further spoil her record by taking a day off without notice. And she knew that one or two hours more could not possibly make up the months of estrangement between them.

"Well, good night."

"Good night." Their hands clung a moment and dropped apart. If only he would say something, do something, she did not know what. But awkwardness held him as it did her.

"Good night." The broad door swung slowly shut behind her. Even then she waited a moment, with a wild impulse to run after him. But she climbed the stairs instead and went wearily to bed, her heart aching with a sense of irreparable loss.

In the morning she was still very tired, and while she drove herself through the day's work she told herself that probably she had never really loved him. "Unless you can love as the angels may, with the breadth of heaven betwixt you," she murmured, remembering the volume of poetry she had found on a library shelf. She had thrilled over it when she read it, dreaming of him; now it seemed to her a grim and almost cynical text. Well, she might as well face a lifetime of work. Lots of women did.

She managed to do this, seeing years upon years of lonely effort, during which she would accumulate money enough to buy a little home of her own. There would be no one in it to criticize her choice of friends or say that she painted her face. That remark clung like a burr in her mind. Yes, she could face a lifetime in which no one would have the right to say things like that!

But when she went home she found that she could not endure an evening of loneliness. Louise and momma were going out, and she was very gay while she dressed to go with them. They said they had never seen her in better spirits.

Unaccountably, the lights, the music, the atmosphere of gaiety, did not get into Rose's blood as usual. At intervals she had moments of depression that they did not touch. She sat isolated in the crowd, sipping her lemon sour, feeling that nothing in the world was worthwhile.

However, she went again the next night. She began to go almost as frequently as momma and Louise, and to understand the unsatisfied restlessness which drove them. She was tired in the mornings, and there were complaints of her work at the office, but she did not care. She felt recklessly that nothing mattered, and she went back to the beach resorts as a thirsty person will sip an emptied glass in which perhaps a drop remains.

"What's the matter, little one? Got a grouch?" said Louise's man, the American Beauty salesman, one night. He was jovial and bald; his neck bulged over the back of his collar, and he wore a huge diamond on his little finger. Rose did not like him, but it was his party. He owned the big red car in which they had come to the beach, and she felt that his impatient reproach was justified. She was not paying her way.

"Not a bit!" she laughed. "Only for some reason I feel like a cold plum-pudding."

"What you need is brandy sauce," Duddy said, appreciating his own wit.

"You mean you want me to get lit up!"

"That's the idea! Bring on the booze, let joy be unrestrained! Waiter, rye highballs all around!"

She did not object; that did not seem worthwhile, either. When the glasses came she emptied hers with the rest, and her spirits did seem to lighten a little. "It removes inhibitions," Gillette Lane had said. And he was gone, too. If he were only here the sparkle of life would come back; she would be exhilarated, witty, alive to her fingertips once more.

The crowd was moving on again. She went with them

into the cool night, and it seemed to her that life was nothing but a moving on from dissatisfaction to dissatisfaction. Squeezed into a corner of the tonneau, she relapsed into silence, and it was some time before she noticed the altered note in the excitement of the others.

"Give her the gas! Let her out! Damn it, if you let 'em pass—!" the car's owner was shouting, and the machine fled like a runaway thing. Against a blur of racing sand dunes Rose saw a long gray car creeping up beside them. "You're going to kill us!" momma screamed, disregarded. Rose on her feet, clinging to the back of the front seat yelled with the others. "Beat him! Beat him! Y-a-a-ay!"

Her hat, torn from her head, disappeared in the roaring blur behind them. Her hair whipped her face. She was wildly, gloriously alive. "Faster, faster!" The gray car was gaining. Inch by inch it crawled up beside them. "Can't you go *faster?*" she cried in a bedlam of shouts. Oh, if only her hands were on the wheel! It was unbearable that they should lose. "Give her more gas, she'll make eighty-five!" the owner yelled.

Everything in Rose narrowed to the challenge of that plunging gray car. Its passing was like an intolerable pulling of something vital from her grip. Pounding her hand against the car door she shrieked frantic protests. "Don't let him do it! Go on! Go on!" The gray car was forging inexorably past them. It swerved. Momma's scream was torn to ribbons by the wind. It was ahead now, and one derisive yell from its driver came back to them. Their speed slowed.

"He's turning in at The Tides. Stop there?" the chauffeur asked over his shoulder.

"Yes, damn you! Wha'd yuh think you're driving, a baby carriage? You're fired!" his employer raged, and he was still swearing when Rose gasping and furious, stumbled from the running-board against Gillette Lane.

"Good Lord, was it you?" he cried. "Some race!" he

exulted and swinging her off her feet, he kissed her gayly. Something wild and elemental in her rushed to meet its mate in him. He released her instantly, and in a chorus of greetings, "Drinks on me, old man!" "Some little car you've got!" "Come on in!" she found herself under a glare of light in the swirl and glitter of The Tides. He was beside her at the round table, and her heart was pounding.

"This is on me!" he declared. "Only my money's good tonight. I'm going to the Argentine tomorrow on the water wagon. What'll you have?"

They ordered, helter-skelter, in a clamor of surprise and inquiry. "Argentina, what're you giving us!" "What's the big idea?" "You're kidding!"

"On the level, Argentina. Tomorrow. Say, listen to me. I've got hold of the biggest proposition that ever came down the pike. Six million acres of land, good land, that'll raise anything from hell to breakfast. Do you know what people are paying for land in California right now? I'll tell you. Five hundred, six hundred, a thousand dollars an acre. And I've got six million acres of land sewed up in Argentina, that I can sell for fifty cents an acre and make— listen to what I'm telling you—and make a hundred per cent profit. The Government's backing me; they'd give me the whole of Argentina. I tell you there's millions in it!"

He was full of radiant energy and power. Rose's imagination leaped to grasp the bigness of this project. Thousands of lives altered, thousands of families migrating, cities, villages, railroads built. She felt his kiss on her lips, and that old, inexplicable, magnetic attraction. The throbbing music beat in her veins like the voice of it. He smiled at her, holding out his arms, and she went into them with recklessness and longing.

They were carried together on waves of rhythm, his arms around her, her loosened hair tumbling backward on her neck.

"I'm mad about you!"

"And you're going away?"

"Sorry?"

"Sorry? Bored. You always do!"

He laughed.

"Not on your life! This time I'm taking you with me."

"Oh, but I wouldn't take you seriously!"

"I mean it. You're coming."

"I'm dreaming."

"I mean it." His voice was almost savage. "I want you."

Fear ran like a challenge through her exultation. She felt herself a small fluttering thing against his breast, while the intoxicating music swept them on through a whirling crowd. His face so close to her was keen and hard, his eyes were reckless as her own leaping blood. "All I've ever needed is a girl like you. You're not going to get away this time."

"Oh, but I'm perfectly respectable!"

"All right! Marry me."

Behind the chaos of her mind there was the tense, suffocating hesitation of the instant before a person leaves the diving-board: security behind him, ecstasy ahead. His nearness, his voice, the light in his eyes, were all that she had been wanting, without knowing it, all these months. The music stopped with a crash.

He stood, as he had stood once before, his arm still tight around her, and in a flash she saw that other time and the dreary months that had followed.

"All right. It's settled?" There was the faintest question in his confident voice.

"You really do love me?"

"I really do." His eyes were on hers, and she saw his confidence change to certainty. "You will!" he said, and kissed her triumphantly, in the crowded room, beneath the glaring lights and crepe-paper decorations. She did not care; she cared for nothing in the world now but him.

"Let's go away a little while by ourselves, out where it's

dark and cool," she said hurriedly as they crossed the floor.

"Not on your life! We're going to have the biggest party this town ever saw!" he answered exultantly over his shoulder, and she saw his enjoyment of the bomb he was about to drop upon the unsuspecting group at the table. "The roof is off the sky tonight. This is a wedding party!"

Louise and momma were upon her with excited cries and kisses, and Rose, flushed, laughing, trying not to be hysterical, heard his voice ordering drinks, disposing of questions of license, minister, ring, rooms at the St. Francis, champagne, supper, flowers. She was the beggar maid listening to King Cophetua.

Part III

Chapter 11

At ten o'clock on a bright June morning Rose Lane tiptoed across a darkened bedroom and closed its door softly behind her. Her tenseness relaxed with a sigh of relief when the door shut with the tiniest of muffled clicks and the stillness behind its panels remained unbroken.

Sunlight streamed through the windows of the living room, throwing a quivering pattern of the lace curtains on the velvet carpet and kindling a glow of ruddy color where it touched mahogany chairs and a corner of the big library table. She moved quickly to one of the broad windows and carefully raised the sash. The low roar of the stirring city rushed in like the noise of breakers on a far away beach, and clean, tingling air poured upon her. She breathed it in deeply, drawing the blue silk negligee closer about her throat.

The two years that had whirled past since she became Gil Lane's wife had taught her many things. She had drawn from her experience generalities on men, women, life, which made her feel immeasurably older and wiser. But there were problems that she had not solved, points at which she felt herself at fault, and they troubled her vaguely while she stood twisting the cord of the window shade in her hand and gazing out at the many-windowed buildings of San Francisco.

She had learned that men loved women for being beautiful, gay, unexacting, sweet-tempered always, docile without being bores. She had learned that men were infuriated by three things: questions, babies, and a woman who was ill. She had learned that success in business depended upon "putting up a front" and that a woman's part was to help in that without asking why or for what end. She had learned that the deepest need of her own nature was to be able to look up to the man she loved, even though she must go down on her own knees in order to do it. She knew that she adored her husband blindly, passionately, and that she dared not open her eyes for fear she would cease to do so.

But she had not quite been able to fit herself into a life with him. She had not learned what to do with these morning hours while he was asleep; she had not learned to occupy all her energies in useless activities while he was away; in a word, she did not know what to do with the part of her life he did not want, and she could not compel herself to be satisfied in doing nothing with it.

Gathering up the trailing silks of her nightgown and negligee she went back to the pile of magazines and books on the table. She did not exactly want to read; reading seemed to her as out of place in the morning as soup for breakfast. But she could not go out, for at any moment Gil might awake and call to her, and she could not dress, for he saw a reproach in that and was annoyed. She turned over the books uncertainly, selecting at last a curious one called *Pragmatism*, which had fascinated her when she dipped into its pages in the library. She had it in her hand when the door bell rang loudly.

She stood startled, clutching the book against her breast. Her heart beat thickly, and the color faded from her face and then poured back in a burning flush. The bell rang again more imperatively. The very sound of it proclaimed that it was rung by a collector. Was it the taxicab man, the tailor, the collection agency? She could not make herself go to the door, and the third long, insistent peal of the bell wrung her like the tightening of a rack. It would waken Gil but what further excuse could she make to the grimly insulting man she visualized on the other side of the door? The bell continued to ring.

After a long time it was silent, and she heard the slam of the automatic elevator's door. A second later she heard Gil's voice.

"Rose! Rose! What the devil?"

She opened the bedroom door and stood smiling brightly on the threshold. "Morning, Gil dear! Behold the early bird's gone with his bill still open!"

"Well, why the hell didn't you open the door and tell him to stop that confounded noise? Were you afraid of disturbing him?"

He knew how it hurt her, but she was trained not to show it. It appeared to her now that she had been criminally selfish in not guarding Gil's sleep. She saw herself a useless incumbrance to her husband's career, costing him a great deal and doing nothing whatever to repay him.

"That's the trouble. It wouldn't have disburbed him a bit!" she laughed bravely. "Somebody ought to catch a collector and study the species and find out what will disturb 'em. I think they're made of cast-iron. I wonder does collecting run in families, or do they just catch 'em young and harden them."

Sometimes even in the mornings talk like this made him smile. But this morning he only growled unintelligibly, turning his head on the pillow. She went softly past the bed into the dressing room.

Gil had scouted her idea of getting an apartment with a kitchenette. He said he had not married a cook, and he hated women with burned complexions and red hands. He made her feel plebeian and common in preferring a home to a hotel. But she had found when she had spent a happy morning buying a coffee percolator and dainty cups and napkins, that he did not mind her giving him coffee in bed. She found a deep pleasure in doing it.

The percolator stood behind a screen in the dressing-room. She turned on the electric switch and, sitting down before the mirror, took off her lace cap and released her hair from its curlers. Gil liked her hair curled. Its dark mist framed a face that she regarded anxiously in the mirror. The features had sharpened a little, and her complexion had lost a shade of its freshness. Gil would insist on her drinking with him, and she knew she must do it to keep her hold on him. A sense of the unreasonableness of men in loving women for their beauty and then destroying it came into her mind, nebulous, almost a thought. But she disregarded it, from a habit she had formed of disregarding many things, and began combing and coiling her hair, carefully inspecting the result from all angles with a hand mirror.

A few minutes later she came into the bedroom, carrying a tray and kicking the trailing lengths of her negligee before her. She held the tray in one hand while she cleared the bedside table with the other, and when she poured the coffee she went through the sitting room and brought in the morning paper. It had been the taxicab man. His bill, stuck in the crack of the door, fluttered down when she opened it, and after glancing at the figures hastily, she thrust it out of sight.

Gil sat up in bed, drinking his coffee, and the smile he gave her made her happy. She curled on the bed beside his drawn-up knees and, taking her own cup from the tray, smiled at him in turn. She never loved him more than at such moments as this, when his rumpled hair and the eyes miraculously cleared and softened by sleep made him seem almost boyish.

"Good?"

"You're a great little chef when it comes to coffee!" he replied. "It hits the spot." He yawned. "Good Lord, we must have had a time last night! Did I fight a chauffeur or did I dream it?"

"It was only a dispute," she said hurriedly.

"That little blond doll was a real looker!"

He could not intend to be so cruel, not even to punish her for letting the bell waken him. It was only that he liked to feel his own power over her. He cared only for women that he could control, and Rose knew that it was the constant struggle between them, in which he was always victorious, that gave her her greatest hold on him. But it did hurt her cruelly in this moment of security to be reminded of the dangers that always threatened that hold.

"Oh, stunning!" Rose agreed, keeping her eyes clear and smiling. She would not fall into the error (and the confession) of being catty. But she felt that Gil perceived her motive, and she knew that in any case he held the advantage over her. She was in the helpless position of the one who gives the greater love.

They sipped their coffee in silence broken only by the crackling of the newspaper. Then, pushing it away, he set down his cup and leaned back against the pillows, his hands behind his head. A moment had arrived in which she could talk to him, and behind her carefully casual manner her nerves tightened.

"It was pretty good coffee," she remarked. "You know, I think it would be fun if we had a real place, with a breakfast room, don't you? Then we'd have grapefruit and hot muffins and all that sort of thing too. I'd like to have a place like that. And then we'd have parties," she added hastily. "We could keep them going all night long if we wanted to in our own place."

He yawned.

"Dream on, little one," he said. But his voice was pleasant.

"Now listen, dear. I really mean it. We could do it. It wouldn't be a bit more trouble to you than a hotel, really. I'd see that it wasn't. I really want it awfully badly. I know you'd like it if you'd just let me try it once. You don't know how nice I'd make it for you.

His silence was too careless to be antagonistic, but he was listening. She was encouraged.

"You don't realize how much time I have when you're gone. I could keep a house running beautifully, and you'd never even see the wheels go round."

"A house!" He was aroused. "Great Scott, doesn't it cost enough for the two of us to live as it is? Don't you make my life miserable whining about bills?"

The color came to her cheeks, but she had never risked letting herself feel resentment at anything he chose to say. She laughed quite naturally. "My goodness!" she said. "You're talking as if I were a puppy! I've never whined a single whine; it's the howling of the collectors you've heard. Let 'em howl; it's good enough for 'em! No, but really, sweetheart, please just let me finish. I've thought it all out. You don't know what a good manager I am." She hurried on, forestalling the words on his lips. "You don't know how much I want to be just a little bit of help. I can't be much, I know. But I'm sure I could save money . . ."

"Old stuff!" he interrupted. "It isn't the money you save: it's the money you make that counts."

"I know!" she agreed quickly. "But we could buy a house, for less than we're paying here in rent. A very nice house. I wouldn't ask you to do it, if it cost any more than we're spending now. But—of course I don't know anything about such things—but I should think it would give you an advantage in business if you owned some property. Wouldn't it make people put more confidence . . ." She faltered miserably at the look in his eyes, and before he could speak she had changed her tactics, laughing.

"I'm just trying to tease you into giving me something I want, and I know I'm awfully silly about it." She nestled closer to him, slipping an arm under his neck. "Oh, honey, it wouldn't cost anything at all, and I do so want to have a house to do things to. I feel so unsettled, living this way. I feel as if I were always sitting on the edge of a chair waiting to go somewhere else. And I'm used to working and managing a little money. I know it wasn't much money, but I liked to do it. You're letting a lot of perfectly good energy go to waste in me, really you are."

He laughed, tightening his arm about her shoulders, and for one deliriously happy moment she thought she had won. Then he kissed her, and before he spoke she knew she had lost.

"I should worry! You're giving me all I want," he said, and there was different delight in the words. She was satisfying him, and for the moment it was enough. He made the mistake of overconfidence in emphasizing a point already won and so losing it.

"As long as I'm giving you three meals a day and glad rags you don't need to worry. I'll look after the finances if you'll take care of your complexion. It's beginning to need it," he added with brutality that defeated its own purpose. Even in her pain she had an instant of seeing him clearly and feeling that she hated him. She rose to her feet and stood trembling, not looking down at him.

"Well, that's settled, then," she said in a clear, hard little voice. "I'll dress. It's nearly noon."

Rose felt that her own anger was threatening the most

precious thing in her life; she felt that she was two persons who were tearing each other to pieces. With a blind instinct of reaching out to him for help she turned at the dressing-room door. "I know you don't realize what you're doing to me; you don't realize what you're throwing away," she said.

There was a cool amusement in his eyes.

"Why the melodrama?" he asked reasonably. She stood convicted of hysteria and stupidity, and she felt again his superiority and his mastery over her.

When Rose came from the dressing-room to find him, careless, good-humored, handsome, tugging his tie into its knot before the mirror, she knew that nothing mattered except that she loved him and that she must hold his love for her. She came close to him, longing for a reassurance that she would not ask. Unless he gave it to her, left her with it to hold in her heart, she would be tortured by miserable doubts and flickering jealousies until he came back. She would be tied to the telephone, waiting for a call from him, trying to follow in her imagination the intricate business affairs from which she was shut out, telling herself that it was business and nothing else that kept him from her.

"Well, bye-bye," he said, putting on his hat.

"Goodbye." Her voice was like a detaining hand. "You won't be gone long?"

"I'm going down to see Stine & Kendrick. I'm going to put through a deal with them that'll put us on velvet," he declared.

"Stine & Kendrick? The real estate people?"

"Yes. We're going to be millionaires when I get through with them!"

The very door seemed to click triumphantly behind him, and she heard his whistling while he waited for the elevator. When he appeared on the sidewalk below, she was leaning from the window, and she would have waved to him if he had looked up. Her occupation for the day vanished when he swung into a streetcar and was carried out of sight.

Rose picked up the pragmatism book again and read a few paragraphs, put it down restlessly. The untidy bedroom nagged at her nerves, but Gil was paying for hotel service, and once when she had made the bed he had told her impatiently that there was no sense in letting the very servants know she was not used to living decently.

She would go for a walk. There might be something new to see in the shop windows. She would take the book with her and read it in the dairy lunchroom where she ate when alone. It seemed criminal to her to spend money unnecessarily when they owed so much, and she could not help trying to save it, though all her efforts seemed to make no difference.

If she could have only a small amount of money regularly, she could manage so much better. Even the salary she had earned as a telegraph-operator sometimes seemed like riches to her, because she had known that she would have it every month and had managed it herself. But every attempt to establish regularity and stability in her present life ended always in the same failure, and she hurriedly turned even her slightest thoughts from the memory of conversations like that just ended.

Rose had been frank with her parents back in Mansfield. Now that times had improved so dramatically for the farm, over Rose's objections they had now and then sent her a little money which she had reluctantly kept, promising herself that it would be returned with interest once the corner was turned in Gillette's affairs. Only last week she'd written them gaily:

Gillette got $18 today, and we nearly threw a fit—the first real money we've seen for ages and ages, except that you sent. So the rent is no more hanging over us like a piece of black crepe—it's funny—here we've been running carefreely around with people who have to hire secretaries to count their money, Gillette has been casually talking millions with men who are as powerful in London as here, and dining at Tait's with champagnè at $12 a bottle, and I went to a lecture in the white and gold room of the St. Francis today at which the cards were $5, and it was an invitation affair besides—and afterward ran into Techau for a bite and saw the check for the four of us—$11—and all the time inside the gnawing mad wish for $20 for the rent man, and the wonder if the gas would be cut off tonight! It is only temporary, of course—that's one of the maddening things about it—and things must loosen up soon and everything will be fine again—

In the dressing room she snapped on all the lights and under the merciless glare critically inspected every line of her face. The carefully brushed arch of the eyebrows was perfect; the slightest trace of rouge was spread skillfully on her cheeks, the round point of her chin, the lobes of her ears. She coaxed loose a tendril of dark hair and wetting it, plastered it against her cheek in a curve that was the final touch of striking artificiality. She did not like it, but Gil did.

She took time in adjusting her hat. Everything depended on that, she knew. She tied her veil with meticulous care. Then, slowly turning before the long mirror set in the door, she critically inspected every detail of her costume: the trim little boots, the crisp, even edges of her skirt, the line of the jacket, the immaculate gloves. A tremendous amount of thought and effort had gone into the making of that smart effect, and she felt that she had done a good job. She would compare favorably with any of the women Gil might meet. A tiny spark of cheerfulness was kindled by the thought. She tried to nourish it, but it went out in dreariness.

What kind of deal was Gil putting through with Stine & Kendrick? It was the first time he had mentioned real estate since the failure of his plan to go to Argentina. That was another memory from which she hastily turned her thoughts, a memory of his alternate moodiness and wild gaiety, of his angry impatience at her most tentative show of interest or sympathy, of their ending an ecstatic, miserable honeymoon by sneaking out of the hotel leaving an upaid bill behind them. She still avoided the hotel, though he must long since have paid the bill. She had not dared ask him, but he had made a great deal of money since then.

There had been the flurry of excitement about the mining stocks, which were selling like wild-fire and promised millions until something happened. And then the scheme for floating a rubber plantation in Guatemala—his long eastern trip and her diamond ring had come out of that—and then the affair of the patent monkey-wrench. He had said that there were millions in it and had derided her dislike of the inventor. She wondered what had become of that enterprise, and secretly thought that she had been right and that the man had tried to swindle Gil.

Now it was real estate again. Rose did not doubt that her clever husband would succeed in it; she was sure that he would be one of America's biggest business men some day, when he turned his genius to one line and followed it with a little more steadiness. But she would have liked to know more about his business affairs. Since they could not have a home yet, she would like to be doing something interesting.

She stopped such thoughts with an impatient little mental shake. Perhaps she would feel better when she had eaten luncheon. With the book tucked under her arm she walked briskly down the sunny wind-swept streets, threading her way indifferently through the tangle of traffic at the corners with the sixth sense of the city dweller, seeing without perceiving them the clanging streetcars, the silent limousines, the streams of cleverly dressed women, preoccupied men, dogs on leashes, and the panorama of shop windows filled with laces, jewels, gowns, furs, hats. She walked surrounded by an isolation as complete as if she were alone in a forest, and nothing struck through it until she paused before a window display.

Rose came to that particular window frequently, drawn by an irresistible attraction. With a pleasant sense of dissipation she stood before it, gazing at glittering bathroom fixtures, rank on rank of shining pans, rows of kitchen utensils, electric flat irons. Today there was a glistening white kitchen cabinet with ingenious flour bin and built-in sifter, hooks for innumerable spoons, sugar and spice jars, an egg beater, a market memorandum device. A tempting yellow bowl stood on a white shelf.

Some day, she thought, she would have a yellow kitchen. She had in mind the shade of yellow, a clear yellow, like sunshine. There would be cream walls and yellow woodwork, at the windows sheer white curtains, which would wash easily, and on the window sill a black jar filled with nasturtiums. The breakfast room should be a glassed-in porch, and its curtains should be thin yellow silk, through which the sunshine would cast a golden light on the little breakfast table spread with a white embroidered cloth and set with shining silver and china. The coffee percolator would be bubbling, and the grapefruit in place, and when she came from the kitchen with the plate of muffins Gil would look up from his paper and say, "Muffins again? Fine! You're the best muffin-maker!"

She dimpled and flushed happily, standing before the unresponsive sheet of plate glass. Then, with a shrug and a half laugh at herself, she came back to reality and went on. But the display held her as a candy shop holds a child, and she must stop again to look at the next window, filled with color cards and cans of paint. Her mind was still busy with color combinations for a living room when she entered the dairy lunch room and carried her tray to a table.

For a moment Rose looked at the crowd about her, clerks and shopgirls and smartly dressed stenographers hurriedly drinking coffee and eating pie. Then she propped her book against the sugar bowl and began slowly to eat, turning a page from time to time. This was an astonishing book. It was not fiction, but it was even more interesting. She read quickly, skipping the few words she did not understand, grasping their meaning by a kind of intuition, wondering why she had never before considered ideas of this kind.

She was so deeply absorbed that she merely felt, without realizing, the presence of someone hesitating at her elbow, someone who moved past her to draw out a chair opposite her and set down his tray. She moved her coffee cup to make room for it, and apologetically lifted the book from the sugar bowl, glancing across it to see Paul.

The shock was so great that for an instant she did not move or think. He stood motionless and stared at her with eyes wiped blank of any expression. Her cup rattled as the book dropped against it and the sound roused her. With the sensation of a desperate twist, like that of a falling cat righting itself in the air, she faced the situation.

"Why, Paul!" she said, and felt that the old name struck the wrong note. "How you startled me. But of course I'm very glad to see you again. Do sit down."

In his face she saw clearly his chagrin, his rage at himself for blundering into this awkwardness, his resolve to see it through. He put himself firmly into the chair and though his face and even his neck were red, there was the remembered determination in the set of his lips and the lift of his chin.

"I'm certainly surprised to see you," he said. "From all I've been hearing about you I had a notion you never ate in places like this any more. They tell me you're getting along fine. I'm mightly glad to hear it." With deliberation he dipped two level spoonfuls of sugar into his coffee and attacked the triangle of pie.

"Oh, I come in sometimes for a change," she said lightly. "Yes, everything's fine with me. You're looking well, too."

There was an undeniable air of prosperity about him. His suit was tailor-made, and the hat on the hook above his head was a new gray felt of the latest shape. His face had changed very slightly, grown perhaps a bit fuller than she remembered, and the line of the jaw was squarer. But he looked at her with the same candid, straight gaze. Of course, she could not expect warmth in it.

"Well, I can't complain," he said. "Things are going pretty well. Slow, of course, but still they're coming."

"I'm awfully glad to hear it. Your mother's well?" The situation was fantastic and ghastly, but she would not escape from it until she could do so gracefully. She formed the next question in her mind while he answered that one.

"Do you often get up to the city?"

"Oh, now and then. I only come when I have to. It's too windy and too noisy to suit me. I just came up this morning to see a real estate firm here about a house they've got in Ripley. I'm going back tonight."

"You're buying a house?" she cried in the tone of a child who sees a toy taken from it. Her anger at her lack of self-control was increased when she saw that he had misinterpreted her feeling.

"Just to rent," he said hastily. "I'm not thinking of moving. Mother and I are satisfied where we are, and I expect it'll be some time before I get that place paid for. This other house . . ." It seemed to her unbearable that he should have two houses. But he went on doggedly, determined, she saw, to give no impression of a prosperity that was not his. "I expect you wouldn't think much of it. But there's a big real estate firm here in San Francisco that's going to boom Ripley, and I wanted to get in on as much of it as I could. They're buying up half the land in the county, and I had an option on a little piece they wanted, so I am trading it for this house. I figure I can fix it up some and make a good thing out of renting it."

She saw that her momentary envy had been absurd. He might have two houses, but he was only one of the unnumbered customers of a big real estate firm. At that moment her husband was dealing as an equal with the heads of such a firm. There was, of course, no comparison between the two men, and she made none. The stirring of remembered affection that she felt for Paul registered in her mind only as a pensive realization of the decay of everything under the erosion of time.

She felt that she was managing the interview very well, and when she saw Paul resugaring his coffee from time to time, with the same deliberate measuring of two level spoonfuls, she felt a complex gratification. She told herself that she did not want Paul to be still in love with her and unhappy, but there was a pleasure in seeing this evidence that his agitation was greater than hers. Being ashamed of the emotion did not kill it.

He told her, with an attempt to control his pride, that he

was no longer with the railroad company. The man who "just about owned Ripley" had given him a better job. He was in charge of the ice-plant and lumber yard now, and he was getting a hundred and fifty a month. He mentioned the figures diffidently, as one who does not desire to be boastful.

"That's fine!" she said, and thought that they paid nearly half that sum for rent, and that the very clothes she was wearing had cost more than his month's salary. She would have liked him to know these things, so that he might see how wonderful Gil was, though they did not have a house, and the cruelty of even thinking this made her hate herself. "Why, you're doing splendidly," she said. "I'm so glad!"

Paul, though conscientiously modest, agreed with her, and was deeply pleased by her applause. After an evident struggle between two opposing impulses, he began to ask questions about her. She found there was very little to tell him. Yes, she was having a very good time. Yes, she was very well. His admiration of her rosy color threw her into a strangling whirlpool of emotions, from which she rescued herself by the sardonic thought that her technique with rouge had improved since their last meeting. She told him vaguely that business was fine, and that they had a lovely apartment on Bush Street.

There was nothing else to tell about herself, and both of them avoided directly mentioning her husband. She had never more keenly realized the emptiness of her life, except for Gil, than when she saw Paul's mind circling about it in an effort to find something there.

He turned at last, baffled, to the book beside her plate.

"Still keeping on reading, I see. Pragmatism? Well, it's all right, I suppose. I don't go much for these Oriental notions about religion, myself."

"It isn't a religion, exactly," she said uncertainly. "It's a new way of looking at things. It's about truth. I mean, it says there isn't any, absolutely, you know," she floundered on before the puzzled question in his eyes. "It says there isn't *absolute* truth. Truth, you know, like a separate thing. Truth's only a sort of quality, like beauty, and it belongs to a thing if the thing works out right. I've got it clear in my head, but I don't express it very well, I know."

"I don't see any sense to it, myself," he commented. "Truth is just simply truth, that's all, and it's up to us to tell it all the time."

She knew that an attempt to explain further would fail, and she felt that her mind had a wider range than his; but she had an impression of his standing sure-footed and firm on the rock of his simple convictions, and she saw that his whole life was as secure and stable as hers was insecure and precarious. She felt about that as she did about his house, envying him something which she knew was not as valuable as her own possessions.

A strange pang, a pain she could not understand, struck her when he stopped at the cashier's grating and paid her check with his own in the most matter-of-fact way.

They parted at the door of the lunch room; for seeing his hesitation she said brightly:

"Well, goodbye. I'm going the other way." She held out her hand, and when he took it she added quickly, "I'm so glad to have seen you looking so well and happy."

"I'm not so blamed happy," he retorted gruffly, as if her words jarred the exclamation from him. He covered it instantly with a heavy, "So I'm glad you are. Goodbye."

That exclamation remained in Rose's mind, repeating itself at intervals like an echo. She had been more deeply stirred than she had realized. Fragments of old emotions, unrealized hopes, unsatisfied longings, rose in her, to be replaced by others, to sink, and come back again. "I'm not so blamed happy." It might have meant anything or nothing. She wondered what her life would be if she were living in a little house in Ripley with him, and rejected the picture, and considered it again.

Looking back, she saw all the turnings that had taken her from the road to a life like that: the road that she had once unquestioningly supposed that she would take. If she had stayed at home in Mansfield; if she had given up the struggle in Sacramento; if she had been able to live in San Francisco with nothing to fill her days but work and loneliness—she saw as a series of merest chances the steps which had brought her at last to Gil.

One could not have everything. She had him. He was not a man who would work slowly, day by day, toward a petty job and a small house bought on the instalment plan. He was brilliant, clever, daring. He would one day do great things, and she must help him by giving him all her love and faith and trust. Suddenly it appeared monstrous that she should be struggling against him, troubling him with her commonplace desires for a commonplace thing like a home, at the very moment when he needed all his wit and skill to handle a big deal. She was ashamed of the thoughts with which she had been playing; they seemed to her an infidelity of the spirit.

Chapter 12

Gil was not in the apartment when Rose reached it; she knew her disappointment was irrational, for she had told herself he would not be there. However, he might telephone. She curled up in the big chair by the window, the book in her lap, and read with a continual consciousness of waiting. She felt that his coming or the sound of his voice would rescue her from something within herself.

At six o'clock she told herself that he would telephone within an hour. Experience had taught her that this way of measuring time helped it pass more quickly. With determined effort she concentrated her attention upon her book, shutting out voices that clamored heart-shaking things to her. At seven o'clock she was walking up and down the living room, despising herself, telling herself that nothing had happened, that he did these things only to show her his hold on her, that at any moment now his message would come.

For another hour she thought of many things she might have done differently. She might have walked past the office of Stine & Kendrick, meeting him as if by accident when he came out. But that might have annoyed him. She might have gone to some of the cafes for tea on the chance of meeting him there. But there were so many cafes! He must be dining in one of them now, and she could not know which one. She could not know who might be dining with him.

"Rose Wilder Lane, stop it! Stop it!" she said aloud. It was the old agony again, and weariness and contempt for herself were mingled with her pain. So many times she had waited, as she was waiting now, and always he had come back to her, laughing at her hysteria. Why could she not learn to bear it more easily? She might have to wait until midnight, until later than midnight. She set her teeth.

The sudden peal of the telephone bell in the dark room startled a smothered cry from her.

"Hello?"

"Rose? Gil. I'm going south tonight on the Lark. Pack my suitcases and ship them express to Bakersfield, will you?"

"What? Yes, right away. Will you be gone long?"

His voice was going on, jubilant:

"Trust your Uncle Gil to put it over! Do you know what I got from the tightest firm in town? An unlimited letter of credit! Get that 'unlimited'?"

"Oh, Gil!"

"It's the biggest land proposition ever put out in the West! Ripley Farmland Acres! I'm going to put them on the map in letters a mile high! Believe me, I'm going to wake things up! There's half a million in it for me if it's handled right, and believe me, I'm some handler!"

"I know you are! Oh Gil, how splendid!"

"All right. Get the suitcases off early—here's my train. So long!"

"Wait a minute—when are you coming back? Can I come, too?"

"Not yet; I'll let you know. Oh, do you want some money?"

"Well, I haven't got much."

"Send you a check. From now on I'm made of money. So long."

"Gil dear," she cried, against the click. Then she slowly put down the telephone. After a moment she went into the bedroom, switched on the lights, and began to pack shirts and collars into his bags. She was smiling, because happiness and hope had come back to her; but her hands shook, for she was exhausted.

It was thirty-two days before Rose heard from him again. A post-dated check for a hundred dollars, crushed into an envelope and mailed on the train, had come back to her, and that was all. But she assured herself that he was too busy to write. The month went by slowly, but it was not unbearably dreary, for she was able to keep uneasy doubts in check, and to live over in her memory many happy hours with him. She planned, too, the details of the house they would have if this time he really did make a great deal of money. He would give her a house, she knew, whenever he could do it easily and carelessly.

When the telephone awakened her one night at midnight her first thought was that he had come back. She was struggling into a negligee when it rang again.

Long distance from Coalinga had a call for her and wished to reverse charges. She repeated the name uncertainly, and the voice repeated: "Call from Mr. Lane in Coalinga."

"Oh, yes, yes! Yes. I'll pay for it. Yes, it's O.K." She waited nervously in the darkness until his voice came faintly to her.

"Hello. Rose! Listen. Have you got any money?"

"About thirty dollars."

"Well, listen Rose. Wire me twenty, will you? I've got to have it right away."

"Of course. First thing in the morning. Are you all right?"

"Am I all right? Good God, Rose! Do you think anybody's all right when he hasn't got any money? We've just got into this rotten burg; been driving all day long and half the night across a desert hotter than the hinges of the main gate, and not a drink for a hundred and forty ..." His voice blurred into a buzzing on the wire, and she caught disconnected words: "Skinflints—over on me—they've got another guess—piker stunt—"

Rose reiterated loudly that she would send the money, and heard central relaying the words. Nothing more came over the wire, though she rattled the receiver. At last she went back to bed, to lie awake till dawn came.

She was waiting at the telegraph office when the money order department opened. After she sent the twenty dollars she drank a cup of coffee, and walked quickly back to the apartment. She felt that she should be able to think of something to do, some action she could take which would help Gil, and many wild schemes rushed through her feverish brain. But she knew that she could do nothing but wait.

The telephone was ringing when she reached her door. It seemed an eternity before she could reach it. Again she assured central that she would pay the charges, and heard Gil's voice. He wanted to know why she had not sent the money, then when she had sent it, then why it had not arrived. He talked a great deal, impatiently, and she saw that his high-strung temperament had been excited to a frenzy by disasters which in her ignorance of business she could not know. Her heart ached with a passion of sympathy and love; she was torn by her inability to help him.

Half an hour later he called again, and demanded the same explanations. Then suddenly he interrupted her, and told her to come to Coalinga. It was a rotten hole, he repeated, and he wanted her.

That he should want her was almost too much happiness, but she tried to be cool and reasonable about it. She pointed out that she had only ten dollars, that it might be wiser, she might be less a burden to him, if she stayed in San Francisco. She would make the ten dollars last, and that would give him time— He interrupted her savagely. He wanted her. Was she coming or was she throwing him over? Thought he couldn't support her, did she? He always had done it, hadn't he? Where'd she get this sudden notion he was no good? He could tell her Gillette Lane wasn't done for yet, not by a damned sight. Was she coming or—

"Oh, yes! yes! yes! I'll come right away! " she cried.

While Rose was packing, she wished that she had something to pawn. The diamond ring had gone when the Guatemala rubber plantation failed; her other jewels were paste or semi-precious stones; her furs were too old to bring anything. She could take Gil nothing but her courage and her faith.

She found that her ticket cost nine dollars and ninety cents. When she reached Coalinga, after a long restless night on the train and a two-hours' careful toilet in the swaying dressing-room, she gave the porter the remaining dime. It was a gesture of confidence in Gil and in the future. She was going to him with a high spirit, matching his reckless daring with her own.

Gil was not on the platform. When the train had gone she still waited a few minutes, looking at a row of one-story ramshackle buildings which paralleled the single track. Obviously they were all saloons. A few loungers stared at her from the sagging board sidewalk. She turned her head, to see on either side the far level stretches of a desert broken only by dirty splashes of sage-brush. The whole scene seemed curiously small under the high gray sky quivering with blinding heat.

She picked up her bags and walked across the street in a

white glare of sunlight. A heavy, sickening smell rose in hot waves from the oiled road. She felt ill. But she knew that it would be a simple matter to find Gil in a town so small. He would be at the best hotel.

She found it easily, a two-story building of cream plaster which rose conspicuously on the one main street. There was coolness and shade in the wide clean lobby, and the clerk told her at once that Gil was there. He told her where to find the room on the second floor.

Her heart fluttered when she tapped on the panels and heard Gil call, "Come in!" She dropped her bags and rushed into a dimness thick with the smoke of cigars. The room seemed full of men, but when the first flurry of greetings and introductions was over and she was sitting on the edge of the bed beside Gil, she saw that there were only five.

They were all young and appeared at the moment very gloomy. Depression was in the air as thick as the cigar smoke. She gathered from their bitter talk that they were land salesmen, that a campaign in Bakersfield had ended in some sudden disaster ("blown up," they said) and that they found a miserable pleasure in repeating that Coalinga was a "rotten territory."

Gil, lounging against the heaped-up pillows on the bed, with a cigar in his hand and whisky and ice water at his elbow, let them talk until it seemed that despondency could not be blacker, then suddenly sitting up, he poured upon them a flood of tingling words. His eyes glowed, his face was vividly keen and alive, and his magnetic charm played upon them like a tangible force. Rose, sitting silent, listening to phrases which meant nothing to her, thrilled with pride while she watched him handle these men, awakening sparks in the dead ashes of their enthusiasm, firing them, giving them something of his own irresistible confidence in himself.

"I tell you fellows this thing's going to go. It's going to go big. There's thousands of dollars in it and every man that sticks is going to be rolling in velvet. Get out if you want to; if you're pikers, beat it. I don't need you. I'm going to bring into this territory the livest bunch of salesmen that ever came home with the bacon. But I don't want any pikers in my game. If you're going to lay down on me, do it now, and get out."

They assured him that they were with him. The most reluctant wanted to know something about details; there was some talk of percentage and agreements. Gil slashed at him with cutting words, and the others bore him down with their aroused enthusiasm. Then Gil offered to buy drinks, and they all went out together in a jovial crowd.

Rose was left alone, to realize afresh her husband's power, and to reflect on her own smallness and stupidity. She stifled a nagging little worry about Gil's drinking. She always wished he would not do it, but she knew it was a masculine habit which she did not understand because she was a woman. After all, men accomplished the big things, and they must be allowed to do them in their own way.

Rose opened the windows, but letting out the smoke let in a stifling heat and the sickening smell of crude oil. She closed them again and reduced the confusion of the room to orderliness, smoothing the bed, gathering up armfuls of scattered papers and unpacking her bags. When Gil came back hours later she was reading with interest a pile of literature about Ripley Farmland Acres.

He came in exuberantly, and as she ran toward him he tossed into the air a handful of clinking gold coins. They fell around her and scattered rolling on the floor. "Trust your Uncle Gil to put one over!" he cried. "Pick 'em up! They're yours!"

"Oh, my dear, my dear!" she gasped, between laughter and the tears that now she could no longer control. Her arms were around his neck. "I knew you'd do it!" she said.

It was a long time before Rose remembered the money. Then, gathering it up, she was astonished to find nearly a hundred dollars. Gil laughed at her when she asked him how he had got it. It was all right. He'd got it, hadn't he? But he told her not to pay for her meals in the dining room, to sign checks instead, and from this she deduced that his business difficulties were not yet entirely overcome. She put the money in her purse, resolving to save it.

She discovered that he now owned a large green automobile. Apparently he had bought it in Bakersfield, for it had been some months since he had sold the gray one. In the afternoon they drove out to the oil leases, and she sat in the car while the salesmen scattered to look for land buyers.

The novelty of the scene was sufficient occupation for her. Low hills of yellow sand, shimmering in glassy heat-waves, were covered with innumerable derricks, which in the distance looked like a weird forest without leaf or shade and near at hand suggested to her grotesque creatures animated by unnatural life, their long necks moving up and down with a chugging sound. There were huddles of little houses, patchworks of boards and canvas, and now and then she saw faded women in calico dresses, or a child sitting half naked and gasping in the hot shadows. She felt that she was in a foreign land, and the far level desert stretching into a haze of blue on the eastern sky line seemed like a sea between her and all that she had known.

The salemen were morose when they returned to the car, and Gil's enthusiasm was forced. "There's millions of dollars a year pouring out of these wells," he declared. "We're going to get ours, boys, believe me!" But they did not respond, and Rose felt an increasing tension while they drove back to town through a blue twilight. She thought with relief of the gold pieces in her purse.

After supper Gil sent her to their room, and she lay in her nightgown on sheets that were hot to the touch while she read of Ripley Farmland Acres. The literature was reassuring; it seemed to her that anyone would buy land so good on such astonishingly low terms. But her uneasiness increased like an intolerable tightening of the nerves, and her enforced inaction in this crisis that she did not understand tortured her. It occurred to her that she was still able to telegraph, and until she dismissed the thought as unfair to Gil she was tantalized by a wild idea of once more having some control of her fate.

It was nearly midnight when he came in, and she saw that any questions would drive him into a fury of irritated nerves. In the morning, she thought, he would be in a more approachable mood. But when she awakened in the dawn he was gone.

Rose did not see him until nearly noon. After sitting for some time in the lobby and exploring as much of the sleepy town as she could without losing sight of the hotel entrance to which he might come, she had returned to the row of chairs beside it and was sitting there when he appeared in the green automobile.

She ran to the curb. He was flushed, his eyes were very bright, and while he introduced her to a man and woman in the tonneau, she heard in his voice the note she had learned to meet with instant alertness. He told her smoothly that Mr. and Mrs. Andrews were interested in Ripley Farmland Acres; he was driving them over to look at the proposition. She leaned across a pile of luggage to shake hands with them and talked engagingly to the woman, but she did not miss Gil's slightest movement or change of expression.

When he asked her to get his driving gloves she knew that he would follow her, and on the stairs she gripped the banister with a hand whose quivering she could not stop.

She was not afraid of Gil in this mood, but she knew that it threatened an explosion of nervous temper as sufficient atmospheric tension threatens lightning. He was at the door of their room before she had closed it.

"Where's that money?"

"Right here." She hesitated, opening her purse. "Gil, it's all we have, isn't it?"

"What difference does that make? It isn't all I'm going to have."

"Listen, just a minute. Did that woman tell you she was going to buy land?"

"Good Lord, do I have to stand here and talk? They're waiting. Give me that money."

"But Gil. She's taking another hat with her. She's got it in a bag, and she's got two suitcases, and the way she looks—I believe she's just going somewhere and getting you to take her in the car. And—please let me finish—if it's all the money we have don't you think—"

She knew that his outburst of anger was her own fault. He was nervous and overwrought; she should have soothed him, agreed with him in anything, in everything. But there had been no time. Shaken as she was by his words, she clung to her opinion, even tried to express it again. She felt that their last hold on security was the money in her purse, and she saw him losing it in a hopeless effort. Against his experience and authority she could offer only an impression, and the absurdity of talking about a hatsack in a woman's hand. The futility of such weapons increased her desperation. His scorn ended in rage. "Are you going to give me that money, or aren't you?"

Tears Rose would not shed blinded her. Her fingers fumbled with the fastening of the purse. The coins slid out and scattered on the floor. Gil picked them up, and the slamming of the door told her he was gone.

She no longer tried to hold her self-control. When it came back to her it came slowly, as skies clear after a storm. Her body was exhausted with sobs and her face was swollen and sodden, but she felt a great relief. She undressed wearily, bathed her face with cool water, and lying down was engulfed in the pleasant darkness of sleep.

The next day and the next passed with a slowness that was like a deliberate refinement of cruelty. She felt that time itself was malicious, prolonging her suspense. The young salesmen shared it with her. They had telegraphed friends and families and were awaiting money with which to get out of town. One by one they were released and departed joyfully. Five days passed. Six. Seven.

Rose would have telegraphed to Stine & Kendrick, but she had no money for the telegram. She would have found work if there had been any that she could do. The manager of the small telegraph office was the only operator. In the little town there were a few stores, already supplied with clerks, a couple of boarding houses on Whiskey Row, and scores of pretty little houses in which obviously no servants were employed. The local paper carried half a dozen "help wanted" advertisements for stenographers and cooks on the oil-leases. She did not know stenography, and she did not have the ability to cook for twenty or forty hungry men.

A bill in her box at the end of the week told her that her room was costing three dollars a day, and she dared not precipitate inquiry by asking for a cheaper one. She was appalled by the prices of the bill-of-fare, and ate sparingly, signing the checks, however, with a careless scrawl and a confident smile at the waitress.

She was coming from the dining room on the evening of the seventh day when the manager of the hotel, somewhat embarrassed, asked her not to sign any more checks for meals. It was a new rule of the house, he said. She smiled at

him, too, and agreed easily. "Why, certainly!" Altering her
intention of going upstairs, she walked into the lobby and
sat relaxed in a chair, glancing with an appearance of
interest at a newspaper.

So it happened that she saw the item in the middle of
the column, which at last gave her news of Gil.

GILLETTE LANE SOUGHT
ON BAD CHECK CHARGE

Charging C. Gillette Lane, well-known along
the city's joy zones, with cashing a bogus check
for a hundred dollars on the Metropolitan
National Bank, Judge C. K. Washburne yesterday issued a warrant for his arrest on a felony
charge. The police search for Lane and his young
wife has so far proved fruitless. Interviewed at his
residence in Los Angeles last night, former Judge
C. G. Lane, father of the missing man, comp-
troller of the Central Trust Company until his
indictment some years ago for mishandling its
funds, denied knowledge of his son's where-
abouts, saying that he had not been on good
terms with his son for several years.

After some time Rose was able to rise and walk quite
steadily across the lobby. Her hand on the banister kept
her from stumbling while she went upstairs. There was
darkness in her room, and it covered her like a shield. She
stood straight and still, one hand pressing against the wall.

It was Saturday night, and in the happy custom of the
oil fields a block of the oiled street had been roped off for
dancing. Already the musicians were tuning their instruments. Impatient drillers and tool-dressers, with their best
girls, were cheering their efforts with bantering applause.

The ropes were giving way before the pressure of the holiday crowd in a tumult of shouts and laughter.

Suddenly, with a rollicking swing, the band began to play. The tune rose gaily through the hot, still night, and beneath it ran a rustling undertone, the shuffling of many dancing feet. Below her window the pavement was a swirl of movement and color. Her body relaxed slowly, letting her down into a crumpled heap, and she lay against the window sill with her face hidden in the circle of her arms.

Chapter 13

Morning came like a change in an interminable delirium. Light poured in through the open window, and the smothering heat of the night gave way to the burning heat of the day. Rose sat up on the tumbled bed, pressing her palms against her forehead, and thought.

The realization of her own position did not rouse any emotion. Her mind stated the situation badly and she looked at it with impersonal detachment. It seemed a curious fact that she should be in a hotel in the oil fields, without money, with no way of getting food, with no means of leaving the place, owing bills that she could not pay.

"Odd that I'm not more excited," she said, and in the same instant forgot about it.

The thought of Gil did not hurt her any more, either. She felt it as a blow on a spot numbed by an anesthetic. But slowly, out of the chaos in her brain, there emerged one thought. She must do something to help him.

She did not need to tell herself that he had not meant to break the law; she knew that. She understood that he had meant to cover the check, that he was in danger because of some accident or miscalculation. In the saner daylight the succession of events that had led to this monstrous catastrophe became clear to her. Gil's overwrought self-confidence when he brought her the gold, his feverish insistence that this was a good territory for land sales, his excitement when he rushed away, believing that he could sell a farm to that shifty-eyed woman with the hat box, should have told her the situation.

Just because Gil had made that tiny mistake in judgment! A frenzy of protest rose in her, beating itself against the inexorable fact. It could not be true that so small an incident had brought such calamity! It was a nightmare. She would not believe it.

"Oh Gil! It isn't true! It isn't—it isn't—Oh Gil!" She stopped that, in harsh self-contempt. It *was* true. "Get up and face it, you coward."

Rose made herself rise, bathed her face and shoulders with cool water. The mirror showed her dull eyes and a mass of frowsy hair stuck through with hairpins. She took out the pins and began tugging at the snarls with a comb. Everything had become unreal; the solid walls about her, the voices coming up from the street below, impalpable things; she herself was least real of all, a shadow moving among shadows. But she must go on; she must do something.

Money. Gil needed money. It was the only thing that stood between him and unthinkable horrors of suffering and disgrace. His father would not help him. Her people could not. Somehow she must get money, a great deal of money.

She did not think out the idea; it was suddenly there in her mind. It was a chance, the only one. She stood at the window, looking out over the low roofs of Coalinga to the sand hills covered with derricks. There was money there. "Millions of dollars a year." She would take Gil's vacant place, sell the farm he had failed to sell, save him.

Her normal self was as lifeless as if it were in a trance,

but beneath its dull weight a small clear brain worked as steadily as the ticking of a clock. It knew Ripley Farmland Acres; it recalled scraps of talk with the salesmen; it reminded her of photographs and blank forms and price lists. She dressed quickly, twisting her hair into a tidy knot, dashing talcum powder on her perspiring face and neck. From Gil's suitcase she hurriedly gathered a bunch of Ripley Farmland Acres literature and tucked it into a salesman's leather wallet. At the door she turned back to get a pencil.

The hotel was an empty place to her. If the idlers looked at her curiously over their waving fans when she went through the lobby she did not know it. It was like opening the door of an oven to meet the white glare of the street, but she walked briskly into it. She knew where to find the livery stable, and to the man who lounged from its hay-scented dimness to meet her she said crisply:

"I want a horse and buggy right away, please."

She waited on the worn boards of the driveway while he brought out a horse and backed it between the shafts. He remarked that it was a hot day; he inquired casually if she was going far. To the oil fields, she said. East or west? "East," she replied at a venture. "Oh, the Limited?" Yes, the Limited, she agreed. When she had climbed into the buggy and picked up the reins, it occurred to her to ask him what road to take.

When she had passed Whiskey Row the road ran straight before her, a black line of oiled sand drawn to a vanishing point on the level desert. The horse trotted on with patient perseverance, the parched buggy rattled behind him, and she sat motionless with the reins in her hands. Around her the air quivered in great waves above the hot yellow sand; it rippled above the black road like the colorless vibrations on the lid of a stove. Far ahead she saw a small dot, which she supposed was the Limited. She would arouse herself when she reached it. Her brain was as motionless as her body, waiting.

She reached the dot, and found a watering trough and an empty house. She unchecked the horse, who plunged his nose eagerly into the water. His sides were rimed with dried sweat, and with the drinking ladle she poured over him water, which almost instantly evaporated. She was sorry for him.

When she was in the buggy again and he was once more trotting patiently down the long road she found that she was looking at herself and him from some far distance, and finding it fantastic that one little animal should be sitting upright in a contrivance of wood and leather, while another little animal drew it industriously across a minute portion of the earth's surface. Her mind became motionless again, as though suspended in the quivering intensity of heat.

An hour later Rose saw that the road was winding over hills of sand. A few derricks were scattered upon them. She stopped at another watering trough, and in the house beside it a faded woman, keeping the screen door hooked between them, told her that the Limited was four miles farther on. It did not occur to her to ask anything more. Her mind was set, like an alarm clock, for the Limited.

She drove into it at last. It was like a small part of a city, hacked off and set freakishly in a hollow of the sand hills. A dozen huge factory buildings faced a row of two-story bunkhouses. Loaded wagons clattered down the street between them, and electric power wires crisscrossed overhead. On the hillside was a group of small cottages, their porches curtained with wilting vines. When Rose had tied the horse in the shade she stood for a moment, feeling all her courage and strength gathering within her. Then she went up the hill.

The screen doors of the cottages opened to her. She

heard herself talking pleasantly, knew that she was smiling, and saw answering smiles. Tired women with lines in their sallow faces tipped the earthen ollas to give her a cool drink, pushed forward chairs for her. Brown-skinned children came shyly to her and touched her dress with sticky little fingers, laughing when she patted their cheeks and asked their names. Mothers showed her white little babies gasping in the heat, and she smiled over them, saying how pretty they were. Beneath it all she felt trapped and desperate.

It seemed to Rose that these women should have started at the sight of her as at a death's head. There was nothing but friendly interest in their eyes, and their obliviousness gave her the comfort that darkness gives to a tortured animal. The hours were going by, relentlessly taking her one hope.

"Do you own any California land?"

"Yes." There would be a flicker of pride in tired eyes. "My husband just bought forty acres last week, near Merced. We're going to pay for it out of his wages, and have it to go to some day!"

"Isn't that fine! Oh yes, the land near Merced is very good land. Your husband's probably done very well. Do you know anyone who's looking for a ranch?" No one did.

She kept on doggedly. When she left each cottage desperation clutched at her throat, and for an instant her breath stopped. But she was so hopeless that she could do nothing but clench her teeth and go on. At the next door she smiled again and her voice was pleasant. "Good afternoon! Might I ask you for a drink of water? Oh, thank you! Yes, isn't it hot? I'm selling farm land. Do you own a California ranch?"

It was when she approached the tenth cottage that the steps, the wilted vine, the little porch went out in blackness before her eyes. But she escaped the catastrophe, and almost at once saw them clearly again and felt the gate post under her tight fingers. The taste in her mouth was blood. She had bitten her lips quite badly, but wiping her mouth with her handkerchief she found that it did not show. She was past caring for anything but finding someone who would buy land. All her powers of thinking had narrowed to that and were concentrated upon it like a strong light on a tiny spot.

In the fourteenth cottage a woman said that she had heard that Mr. MacAdams, who worked in the boiler factory, had been to Fresno to buy land and had not bought it. Rose thanked her, and went to the boiler factory.

It was a large building, set high above the ground. Circling it, she saw a man in overalls and undershirt lounging in a wide doorway above her. The roar and bang and whir of machinery behind him drowned her voice, and he stared at her as at an apparition. When he leaped down beside her and understood her demand to see Mr. MacAdams the expression of perplexity changed to a broad grin. MacAdams was in a boiler, he said, and still grinning, he climbed back to the door step and drew her up by one arm into a huge room shaking with noise. He led her through crashing confusion and with his pipe stem pointed out MacAdams.

MacAdams was crouching in a big cylinder of steel. In his hand he held a jerking riveter, and the boiler vibrated with its racket. His ears were stuffed with cotton, his eyes intent on his work. In mute show Rose thanked the man beside her and, going down on her hands and knees, crawled into the boiler. When she touched MacAdams' shoulder the riveter stopped.

"I beg your pardon," she said. "I heard you were interested in buying a ranch."

MacAdams' astonishment was profound. Mechanically

he put a cold pipe in his mouth and took it out again. She saw that his mind was passive under the shock. Sitting back on her heels she opened the wallet and took out the pictures. Her voice sounded thin in her ears.

"There's lots of good land in California. I wouldn't try to tell you, Mr. MacAdams, that ours is the only land a man can make money by buying. But what do you think of that alfalfa?"

She knew that it was alfalfa because the picture was so marked on the back. While he looked at it she studied him, and her life was blank except for his square Scotch face, the deliberate mind behind it, and her intensity of purpose.

Rose saw that she must not talk too much. His mind worked slowly, standing firmly at each point it reached. He must think he was making his own decisions. She must guide them by questions, not statements. He would be obstinate before definite statements. He was interested. He handed back the picture and asked a question. She answered it from the information in the advertising, and while she let him reach for another picture she thought quickly that she must not let him catch her in a lie. If he asked a question, the answer to which she did not know, she must say so. She was ready when it came.

"I don't know about that," she answered. "We can find out on the land if you want to go and look at it."

He was noncommittal. She let the point go. She felt that her life itself hung on his decisions, and she could do nothing to hasten them. Her hands were shaking, and she forced her body to relax. She unfolded a map of Ripley Farmland Acres and pointed out the proposed railroad, the highway, the irrigation canals. She made him ask why part of the map was painted red, and then told him that those farms were sold. He was impressed. She folded the map a second too soon, leaving his interest unsatisfied.

He said he thought the proposition was worth looking

into. She did not reply because she feared her voice would not be steady. In the pause he added that he would go over and look at it next Tuesday. She unfolded the map again. Her fingers were cold and stiff paper rattled between them, but the moment had come to test her success, and she would not deceive herself with false hopes.

She told him that she wanted to reserve a certain farm for him to see. She pointed it out at random. It was a very good piece, she said, the best piece unsold. She feared it would be sold before Tuesday. It could not be held unless he would pay a deposit on it. If he did not buy it the deposit would be returned.

"You don't want to waste your time, Mr. MacAdams, and neither do I." She felt the foundations of her self-control shaking, but she went on, looking at him squarely. "If this piece suits you, you will buy it, won't you?"

He would. If it suited him.

"Then please let me hold it until I can show it to you."

She waited while time ticked by slowly. Then he leaned sidewise, putting his hand in his pocket. "How much will I have to put up?"

When Rose backed out of the boiler five minutes later she had a twenty-dollar gold piece in her hand, and in her wallet was the yellow slip of paper with his signature on the dotted line. She stumbled down a lane between whirring machinery and dropped over a door sill into the hot dust of the road. Her grip on herself was being shaken loose by unconquerable forces. She ran blindly to the buggy, and when she had somehow got into it she heard herself laughing through sobs in her throat. The horse trotted gladly toward Coalinga.

During the long drive across the desert she sat relaxed, too weary to be troubled or pleased by anything. The sun sank slowly beyond cool blue hills, and darkness crept down from them across the level miles of sand. A crescent of twinkling lights appeared on the lower slopes, where the western oil fields lay. Their lower rim was Coalinga, and she thought of bed and sleep. Clutching the gold piece, she reminded herself that she must eat. She must keep up her strength until she had sold that piece of land. She was too tired to face that effort now. The horse took her quickly past Whiskey Row and dashed to the livery stable. She climbed down stiffly.

"Charge it." Her voice was stiff, too. "Stine & Kendrick, San Francisco. I'm representing them. R. W. Lane; I'm at the hotel."

Her body lagged as she drove it to the telegraph office. She had written a telegram to Stine & Kendrick before she realized that she dared not face any inquiry until after Tuesday. It occurred to her then that she had committed a crime. She was not certain what it was, but she thought it was obtaining money under false pretenses. She destroyed the telegram.

Later, when Rose laid the twenty-dollar gold piece on the check for her supper, it seemed to her that she was embezzling. A discrepancy vaguely irritated her. Could one obtain money under false pretenses and then embezzle it, too? She was too tired to be deeply concerned, but as an abstract question it annoyed her. The waitress looked at her sharply, and she wondered if she had said something about it. In a haze she got up the stairs and into bed.

Chapter 14

Very early Tuesday morning Rose drove to the Limited lease and got MacAdams. He looked formidable in his good clothes, and now that he had shaved the scrubby gray beard his chin had an even more obstinate line. She talked to him in an easy and friendly manner, without mentioning land. She must not waste her strength. There was a struggle before her and a menace behind. She had opened a livery stable account against Stine & Kendrick, who had never heard of her. The hotel, she knew, had let her go only because she took no baggage and had told the clerk casually that she would return tomorrow. The ticket to Ripley left five dollars of the twenty that belonged to MacAdams. And every moment that the sale was delayed might make it impossible to save Gil.

She sat smiling, listening to a tale of MacAdams' youth, when he was a sea-faring man.

The train reached Fresno, and MacAdams' gaze rested with joy on leafy orchards and vineyards and the cool green of alfalfa fields. She perceived the effect upon him of that refreshing contrast with the arid desert. Before they reached Ripley his mind would be adjusted to a green land and ditches filled with running water. She had lost one point.

Her attention concentrated upon the thoughts slowly forming in his mind. Each word he spoke was an indication which she seized, considered, turned this way and that, searching for the roots of it, the implications growing from it.

The train was now running across a level plain covered with dry grass. Desolation was written upon it, and small unpainted houses stood here and there like periods at the end of sentences expressing the futility of human hope. She smiled above a sinking heart. They alighted at Ripley.

Rose had never seen the town before, and she saw now, with MacAdams' eyes, a yellow station, several big ware-houses, a wide dusty road into which a street of two-story buildings ran at right angles. It was not much larger than Coalinga. She looked anxiously for the agent from Ripley Farmland Acres. That morning she had telegraphed him to meet her.

He came toward them and shook MacAdams' hand heartily. His name was Nichols. He had a consciously frank eye, and a smooth manner. He hustled them toward a dusty automobile whose sides were covered with canvas advertisements of the tract, and put MacAdams into the front seat beside him.

The machine, stirring a cloud of dust behind it, rattled down the road between fields of dry stubble. She was ignored in the back seat. Nichols had taken the situation out of her hands, and she did not trust him. However, she could not trust herself, in the midst of her uncertainties and ignorance.

Nichols talked too much and too enthusiastically. She was astounded by his blindness. To her it seemed obvious that his words were of little importance. It was what MacAdams said that mattered. He gave MacAdams no silences in which to speak, and he appeared oblivious to the fact that MacAdams, gazing contemplatively at the sky line, said nothing.

They drove beneath an elaborate plaster gateway into the tract. Seventy thousand acres of scorched dry grass lay before them, stretching unbroken to a misty level horizon. Over it was the great arch of a hot sky.

The car carried them out into the waves of dry grass like the smallest of boats putting out into an ocean of aridity. When it stopped the sun poured its heat upon them and dust settled on perspiring hands and faces. Nichols unrolled a map and talked with galvanic enthusiasm. He talked incessantly and his phrases seemed worn threadbare by previous repetition. MacAdams said nothing, and Rose tried to devise a way to ask Nichols to stop talking.

His manner had dropped her outside of consideration, save as a woman for whom automobile-doors must be opened. She saw that he felt her presence as a handicap in this affair between men; he apologized for saying "damn," and his apology conveyed resentment. He was losing her the sale, and she could not interfere. Her only hope of saving Gil rested on this sale. She controlled a rising desperation, and smiled at him.

They got out of the car and waded through dusty grass, searching for surveyor's posts. Nichols pointed out the luxuriant growth of wild hay, asked MacAdams what he thought of that, continued without a pause to pour facts and figures upon him, heedless that he received no reply. They got into the car again, and Nichols, pulling a pad of blanks from his pocket, tried to make MacAdams buy a certain piece of land then and there. He attacked obliquely, as if expecting to trap MacAdams into signing his name, and MacAdams answered as warily. "Well, I have seen worse. And I have seen better." He lighted his pipe and listened equably. He did not sign his name.

They drove further down the road and got out again.
Rose caught Nichols' sleeve, and though he shook his arm
impatiently she held him until MacAdams had walked
some distance away and picked up a lump of soil.

"Leave him to me, please," she said.

"What do you know about the tract?"

"Just the same, I want you to give me the chance,
please."

"Do you want to sell him or don't you? I know how to
handle prospects."

They spoke quickly. Already MacAdams was turning his
head.

"He's my prospect. And, by God! I'm going to sell him
or lose him myself!" Her words shocked her like a
thunderclap, but the shock steadied her. And Nichols'
overthrow was complete. He said hardly a word when they
reached MacAdams.

Almost in silence they examined that piece of land.
MacAdams walked to each of its corners; he looked at the
map for some time; he asked questions that Nichols
answered briefly. He pulled up clumps of grass and looked
at the earth on their roots. At last he walked back to the
machine and leaned against it, lighting his pipe leisurely
and looking out across the tract. The silence was palpitant.
When she saw that he did not mean to break it, Rose
asked, "Shall we look at another piece?"

"No, I've seen enough."

They got into the car, and this time Nichols was alone in
the front seat. They drove back toward the tract office. The
sun was sinking, and a gray light lay over the empty fields.
Rose felt herself part of it. She had lost, and nothing
mattered any more. She had no more to lose. She kept up
the hopeless effort, but the approaching end was like the
thought of rest to a struggling man who is drowning.

"What do you think of it, Mr. MacAdams?"

"Well, I have seen worse."

"Were you satisfied with the soil?"

"I wouldn't say anything against it."

"Would you like us to show you anything more of the water system?" What did she care about water systems!

"No."

The car stopped before the tract office. They got out.

"Your man's no good. He's a looker, not a buyer," Nichols said to her in an aside.

"He has money and he wants land," she answered wearily.

"We'll have another go at him. But it's no use."

They went into the office. A smoky kerosene lamp stood on a desk littered with papers. MacAdams asked when the train left Ripley. Nichols told him that they had half an hour. They sat down, and Nichols, drawing his chair briskly to the desk, began.

"Now, Mr. MacAdams, in buying land you have to consider four things: land, water, climate, and markets. Our land . . ."

She could not go back to Coalinga with him. Probably there would be a warrant out for her arrest. Oh, Gil! She had done her best, her very best. There were five dollars left, MacAdams' money. The whole thing was unreal. She was dreaming it.

Nichols was leading him up to the decision. MacAdams evaded it. Nichols began again. The blank form was out now and the fountain pen ready.

"You like the piece, don't you? You're satisfied with it. You've found everything exactly as we presented it. It's the best buy on the tract. Well, now we'll just close it up."

MacAdams put his hands in the pockets and gazed at the map on the wall. "I'm not saying it isn't a good proposition."

Nichols began again. Was forty acres more than Mac-

Adams wanted to carry? MacAdams would not exactly say that. Would a change in the terms be more convenient for him? MacAdams had no fault to find with the terms. Did the question of getting the land into crop trouble him? No. Well, then they'd get down to the point. "I'll not be missing my train, Mr. Nichols?"

Patiently Nichols went back to the beginning. Land, water, transportation, and climate. Rose could endure it no longer. One straight question would end it, would leave her facing certainty. She leaned forward and heard her own voice.

"Mr. MacAdams, you came to look at this land. You've looked at it. Do you want it?"

There was one startled, arrested gesture from Nichols. Then they remained motionless. The clock ticked loudly. Slowly MacAdams leaned back in his chair, straightened one leg, put his hand into his trouser pocket. He pulled out a grimy canvas bag.

"Yes. How much is the first payment?"

Deliberately he poured out on the desk a heap of golden coins. His stubby fingers extracted from the sack a wad of banknotes. Nichols was figuring madly. "Twelve hundred and seventy-three dollars and ninety cents," he announced in a shaking voice. MacAdams counted it out with exactness. He signed the contract. Nichols recounted the money and sealed it in an envelope. They rose.

Rose found herself stumbling against the side of the automobile, and felt Nichols squeezing her arm exultantly while he helped her into it. They had reached Ripley before she was able to think. Then she said that she would not return to Coalinga with MacAdams. They put him on the train.

She told Nichols that she wanted the money and the contract. She was going to take the next train to San

Francisco. He objected. She argued through a haze, and her greatest difficulty was keeping her voice clear. But she held tenaciously to her purpose. Later she was on the train with the contract and Nichols' check drawn to Stine & Kendrick. She slept then and she slept in the taxicab on the way to a San Francisco hotel. She felt that she was asleep while she wrote her name on a register. She shut a door somehow behind a bell boy, and at last could sleep undisturbed.

At nine o'clock the next morning she sat facing Mr. Stine across a big flat-topped desk. The contract and Nichols' check lay upon it.

Mr. Stine was a lean, shrewd-looking man about forty-five years old. He gave the impression of having kept his nerves at high tension for so many years that now he must strain them still tighter or relax altogether. This catastrophe he would have described as "losing his grip," and Rose felt that he lived in dread of it as the ultimate calamity. They had been talking for some time. Mr. Stine did not know where Gil was.

"My dear young lady, if we had known . . ." he said and he stopped because it would be useless cruelty to complete the sentence. She thought that he would not be cruel unless there were some purpose to be achieved by it. There was even a kindly expression in his eyes at times.

He had explained clearly the situation in which her husband stood. Gil had persuaded the firm to give him an unlimited letter of credit. "That young man has a truly remarkable personality as a salesman. He had us completely up in the air." He had proposed a gigantic selling campaign in the oil fields, and had so filled Stine & Kendrick with his own enthusiasm that they had given him free rein.

The campaign had begun with every promise of astounding success. He had brought huge crowds to hear speakers sent down from the city; had gathered the names of thousands of "leads"; had imported fifty salesmen to canvass these names and bring in prospective buyers. Scores of these had been taken to the land and hundreds more were promised. Stine & Kendrick contemplated hiring special trains for them.

But expenses were running into disquieting amounts for the actual results produced. Gil's checks poured in, and there began to be annoying rumors. The firm had begun a quiet investigation and had decided that he was spending too much of their money for personal expenses. Mr. Stine need not go into details. They had withdrawn the letter of credit and advised creditors in Bakersfield that the firm would no longer pay Mr. Lane's bills.

Mr. Lane had been informed of this. He had taken one of the firm's automobiles and disappeared. Later his check had come in. Stine & Kendrick could not make that good, in addition to their other losses. The matter was now entirely out of their hands. Mr. Stine's gesture placed it in the hands of inscrutable fate. He was more interested in the MacAdams sale and the unexpected appearance of Rose.

However, under her insistence he admitted that if the check were made good, Stine & Kendrick could persuade the bank not to press the charge. Of course the warrant was out, but there were ways. He would undertake to employ them for her, he said, thoughtfully fingering Nichols' check. As to finding Gil—well, the police had failed.

Rose asked how much Gil owed the firm. Mr. Stine told her that the sum was roughly five thousand dollars.

"In thirty days! How is it possible?"

The amount included the cost of the automobile. The balance was Mr. Lane's personal expenses, not included in his arrangement with the firm. "Wine, ah—" Mr. Stine did not complete the trilogy. "Mr. Lane's recreations were expensive." He would have the account itemized?

"Oh, no. It isn't necessary," said Rose. She would like to know only the exact sum. Mr. Stine pressed a button and asked the girl who answered it to look up the amount. "And, by the way, have this sale entered on the books, and a check made out to?"

"R. W. Lane," said Rose.

"To R. W. Lane for the commissions. Seven and a half percent."

"You are paying the other salesmen fifteen percent," said Rose.

That was by special arrangement. The ordinary salesmen in the field were paid seven and a half percent. Rose accepted the statement, being unable to refute it. She proposed that she should continue working for the firm on twelve and a half percent, five percent to apply on the amount Gil owed them. Mr. Stine countered with the fact that no California firm had ever engaged a woman real estate agent and offered her ten percent with the same arrangement. She was stubborn, and he yielded.

Rose came out of the office with three hundred dollars in her purse. She saw that the sun was shining, and as she walked through the crowded, familiar streets, passing flower stands gay with color, feeling the cool breeze on her face, and seeing white clouds sailing over Twin Peaks, she felt that the bright day was mocking her.

Her life was beginning again, in a new way, among strange surroundings. She thought that it would be pleasant to be dead. One would be then as she was, numb, with no emotion, no interest, no concern for anything, and one would not have to move or think. "Cheer up! What's the use of wishing you were dead? You will be some day!" she said to herself, with an effort to be humorous about it.

She thought that she would go out to the old apartment,

pack the things she had left there, and take them with her. There was a hard bitterness in the thought that seemed almost sweet to her. To stand unmoved in that place where she had loved and suffered, to handle with uncaring hands those objects saturated with memories, would be a desecration of the past that would prove how utterly dead it was.

But she did not do it. She telephoned from the station, giving up the apartment and abandoning the personal belongings in it, leaving her address for the forwarding of mail. Then she shut her mind against memories and went back to the oil fields.

Chapter 15

During the weeks that followed Rose felt that she was
moving in a dream, a shadow among unrealities. She drove
across endless yellow plains that wavered in the heat. The
lines were lax in her hands; her thoughts hardly moved.
Again she had the sensation of gazing upon herself from an
infinite distance, and she saw her whole life very small and
far away and unimportant.

She thought: It was odd that she should be where she
was. They would reach the watering trough soon, and then
the horse could drink. The lake she saw rippling upon the
burning sand was a mirage. The horse was not interested in
it. Horses must recognize water by smelling it. The sunlight
struck her hands, and they were turning browner. Complexions. How strange that women cared about them. How
strange that anyone cared about anything.

Rose reached an oil lease, and part of her brain awoke. It
worked so smoothly that she felt an impersonal pride in it.
It was concerned only with Ripley Farmland Acres. It was
intent upon selling them. She tapped at screen doors, and
knew she was being charming to tired women exhausted by
heat and babies. She skirted black pools of oil, climbed into
derricks (she had learned to call them "rigs") and heard

herself talking easily to grimy men beside a swaying steel cable that went eternally up and down, up and down, in the well-shaft.

Selling land, she found, was not the difficult and intricate business she had supposed it to be. California's great estates, the huge Mexican grants of land now passed to the second and third generations, were breaking up under the pressure of growing population and increased land taxes; for the first time in the state's history the land hunger of the poor man could be satisfied. Deep in the heart of every person imprisoned by those burning wastes of desert was the longing for a small bit of green earth, a home embowered in trees and vines. Her task was to find the workman who had saved enough money for the first payment, the ten or twenty per cent of the purchase price asked by the subdividing land companies, and having found him to play upon his longing and his imagination until the pictures she painted meant more to him than his hoarded savings.

Half of the buyer's first payment was hers; one sale meant to her five hundred or even a thousand dollars. But while she talked she forgot this; she thought only of cool water flowing through fields of alfalfa, of cows knee-deep in grass beneath the shade of oaks, of the fertile earth blooming in harvests. The skill in handling another's thoughts before they took form, learned in her life with Gil, enabled her to impress these pictures upon her hearer's mind so that they seemed his own, and grimy men in oil-soaked overalls, listening to her without combativeness because she was a woman and not to be taken seriously in business, felt that they must buy this land so temptingly described.

"I'm not really a land salesman," Rose said, believing it. "I know I can't *sell* you this land. I can only tell you about

it. And then if you want to buy it, you will. Won't you?"
She found that she need only talk to a sufficient number of
men to find one who would buy, and each sale brought her
enough money to give her weeks in which to trudge from
derrick to derrick searching for another buyer. All her life
had narrowed to that search.

She accumulated a store of facts. Drillers were the best
prospects because they earned good salaries and had
steady, straight-thinking brains. Tool dressers were younger men, inclined to smartness, harder to handle. Pumpers
were lonely and liked to talk; one must not waste too much
time on them; they made small wages, but would give her
"leads" to good prospects. A superintendent of a wild-cat
lease was a good prospect; approach him with talk of a safe
investment. Shallow fields were poor territory to work; jobs
were longer and wages surer among the deeper wells. At a
house ask for a drink of water; on a rig begin conversation
by remarking, "Getting pretty deep, isn't she?" She was
known throughout the fields as the Real Estate Lady.

At twilight she drove back to the hotel. Her khaki skirt
was spattered with crude oil; her pongee waist showed
streaks of grime where dust had dried in perspiration.
There was sand in its folds, sand in her shoes, sand in her
hair. Her body seemed as lifeless as her emotions, and her
brain had stopped again. She would not dream tonight.

She smiled again at the hotel clerk, Yes, thank you,
business was fine! There were letters, no word of Gil. Her
mother wrote puzzled and anxious inquiries. What was
Rose doing in Coalinga? Was something wrong? What was
her husband doing? Mrs. Updike was telling that she had
seen in the paper . . . Rose folded the pages. There were a
couple of thin envelopes from Stine & Kendrick, an-
nouncements of sales. Farm 406—J. D. Hutchinson; Farms
915-917—R. W. Lane.

It was good to be in bed, feeling unconsciousness creeping over her like dark, cool water, lapping higher and higher.

On her third trip to the land with buyers Rose met Paul's mother on the main street in Ripley. Mrs. Masters appeared competent and self-assured, walking briskly from a butcher shop with some packages on her arm. She was bareheaded, carrying a parasol above her smooth, gray hair. Small as she was, there was something formidable in the lines of her sturdy figure and in the crispness of her stiff white shirtwaist. She looked at Rose with shrewd, interested eyes, and Rose realized that her hair was untidy, that there was dust on her shoes and on her blue serge suit. It was dust from the tract where she had just made another sale. Rose supposed there was dust on her face, too, when she perceived Mrs. Masters' eyes fixed so intently upon it.

They shook hands and spoke of the heat. Rose explained that she was selling land. She had just put one buyer on the Coalinga train and was waiting in Ripley for another man to meet her next day.

Mrs. Masters asked her to supper. A realization that meeting her might be embarrassing to Paul flickered through Rose's mind. She made some excuse, which Mrs. Masters overruled briskly. The strain of making a sale had left Rose without energy for resistance. She found they were walking down the street together, and she tried to rouse herself, as one struggles under an anesthetic. Mrs. Masters was the first person to whom she had tried to talk of anything but land, and the effort made her realize that she had been living in a delirium.

They came to the cottage of which Paul had written her long ago. There was the little white picket fence, the yard with rose bushes in it, and the peach tree. The graveled walk led to a tiny porch ornamented with wooden lace

work, and through a screen door they went into the parlor.
The shades were drawn to keep the afternoon sun from the
flowered Brussels carpet; the room was cool and dim and
rose-scented. There was a crocheted mat on the oak center
table; cushions stood stiff and plump on the sofa; in one
corner on an easel was an enlarged crayon portrait of Paul
as a little boy.

There was not a detail of the room that Rose would not
have changed, but as she looked at it tears came unexpectedly into her eyes. Something was here that she wanted,
something that she had always missed. Currents of emotion
rose in her. Her heart ached, and suddenly she was shaken
by a sense of irretrievable loss.

"I'm very tired. You must forgive me; it's been a very
hard day. Might I lie down a minute?" She stopped the
quivering of her lips. Mrs. Masters looked at her curiously,
leading her to the bedroom and folding back an immaculate white spread. Rose, hating herself for her weakness,
took off her hat and lay down. She would be all right in a
minute; she was sorry to make so much trouble; Mrs.
Masters must not bother; she was just a little tired.

She lay still, hearing the rattling of pans and sizzling of
meat from the kitchen where Mrs. Masters was getting
supper. Voices went by in the street; a dog barked joyously;
a shrill whistling passed, accompanied by the rattle of a
stick along the picket fence. The sharp shadows of vine
leaves on the shade blurred into the twilight. Mrs. Masters
was singing throatily, "Rock of Ages, cleft for me-e-e,"
while she set the table.

It was peace and security and rest. It was all that Rose
did not have. The papered walls enclosed a haven warmed
by innumerable homely satisfactions. How sweet to have
no care but the crispness of curtains, the folding away of
linen, the baking of bread! She was an alien spirit here,

with her aching head and heart, her disheveled hair and dusty shoes. A tear slipped down her cheek and spread into a damp splash on the white pillow.

Rose got up quickly, knowing that she must be stronger than the longing that shook her. The towel lying across the water pitcher was embroidered. She had always wanted embroidered towels, and she had made dozens of them. They had been left in the apartment. She bathed her face for a long time, dashing cool water on her eyelids.

The gate clicked, and Paul came whistling up the path. She stood clutching the towel, shivering with panic. Had she been mad to have come to his house? Oh, for anything, anything, that would erase the past hour, and let her be anywhere but here! She heard his step on the porch, the bang of the screen door, his voice. "Hello, mother? Supper ready?" And at the same time she saw unrolling in her mind the picture of herself and Mrs. Masters on the sidewalk, heard the definite, polite excuse she might have made, saw herself going back to the hotel. She might easily have done that. Why was her life nothing but a continuing blundering stupidity? She waited until his mother had time to tell him she was there. Then she went out, smiling, and met him.

Paul's hand was warm and strong, closing around her cold fingers. He could not conceal the shock her whiteness and thinness gave him. He stammered something about it, and reddened. She saw that he felt he had referred to Gil and hurt her. Yes, she said lightly, the heat in the oil fields was fierce; she rather liked it, though. And selling land was fascinating work. She found that she was clinging to his hand, drawing strength from it, as though she could not let go. She released her fingers quickly, hoping he had not noticed that second's delay, which meant nothing, nothing except that she was tired.

Mrs. Masters sat opposite her at the supper table, and with those polite, neutral eyes upon her it was hard to make conversation. She told the story of the MacAdams sale, making it humorous, trying to keep the talk away from Mansfield and the people there. Paul spoke only to offer her food, to advise a small glass of his mother's blackberry cordial and urge her to drink it, to suggest a cushion for her back. Tears threatened her eyes again, and she conquered them with a laugh.

He went with her to the hotel. They walked in silence through moonlight and shadow, on the tree-bordered graveled sidewalk. Through lighted cottage windows Rose saw women clearing supper tables, men leaning back in easychairs, with cigar and newspaper. They passed groups of girls, bare-headed, bare-armed, chattering in the moonlight. They spoke to Paul, and Rose felt their curious eyes upon her. Children were playing in the street; somewhere a baby wailed thinly, and farther away a piano tinkled.

"All of this is very lovely," Rose said.

"It suits me," Paul replied. A little later he cleared his throat and said, "Rose, I'm sorry."

"I'm all right," she said quickly. It was almost as if she had slammed a door in his face, and she did not want to be rude to him. "It's good of you to care. I'd rather not talk about it."

"I sometimes think I could commit murder!" he said thickly. "When I get to thinking . . ."

"Don't," Rose said. It was some time before he spoke again.

"Well, if there is ever any chance for me to do anything, I guess you know I'd be glad to."

She thanked him. When he left her at the door of the hotel she thanked him again, and he asked her not to forget. If he could help her with her sales or the bank people or anything. She said she would surely let him know.

It was necessary to sleep, because she had another sale, a hard sale, to make next day. But she was unable to do it. Long after midnight she was lying awake, beating the pillows with clenched hands and biting her lips to keep from sobbing aloud. It seemed to her that all of life was torture and that she could no longer bear it.

Chapter 16

Returning to Coalinga after meeting Paul, Rose ached with weariness. But she was alive again. The haze in which she had been existing was gone. She had risen early that morning, met her prospective land buyer at the train, and made the sale. It had been doubly difficult, because the salesman for Alfalfa Tracts had met the train, too, and had almost taken the prospect from her, thinking it would be easy to do because she was only a woman. There was a hard triumph in her victory. The sale had reduced Gil's debt by another four hundred dollars, for she could afford now to turn in the entire commission against it.

The jolting of the train shook her relaxed body. Her cheek lay against the rough plush of the chair-back, for she was too tired to sit upright. Against the black square of the window her life arranged itself before her. How many times she had seen her life lying before her like a straight road, and had determined what its course and end would be! But she was older now, and wiser, and able to control her destiny.

She was a land salesman; she was a good salesman. This was the only thing she had saved from wreckage. At least she would succeed in this. She would make money; she would clear Gil's name, which was hers; she would buy a little house and make it beautiful. Perhaps Gil would want to come to it some day. She knew that she would never love him as she had loved him, for she saw him too clearly now, but she felt that their lives were inextricably bound together.

A letter from Stine & Kendrick was in her box at the hotel. It said that the firm had given the oil fields territory to two other salesmen, Hutchinson and Monroe. The oil fields had proved a good territory, and it was too large for her to handle alone. She would turn over to Hutchinson and Monroe any leads she had not followed up. Doubtless she could make arrangements with them as to commissions; the firm hoped she would continue to work in the fields; Hutchinson and Monroe would expect an overage on her sales. Mr. Stine trusted they would work in harmony, and congratulated her on her success.

Rose's first astonishment changed quickly to a cold rage. Did they think they could take her territory from her? Her territory, that she had developed herself, alone? After her days and weeks of hard, exhausting work, after her hours of talking, of distributing advertising, of making sales that would lead to more sales, they were coming in and taking the fruits of it away from her? Oh, would she fight!

The clerk told her that Hutchinson and Monroe had arrived that afternoon. She asked him to tell them that she would see them in the parlor at nine o'clock. There would be some slight advantage in making them come to her.

Rose was sitting in the small, stuffy room, her eyes fixed on a newspaper, when they came in. She felt hard, like a machine of steel, when she rose smiling to meet them.

Hutchinson was a tall, angular man, who moved in an easy-going way as if his body had nothing to do with the loose-fitting, gray clothes he wore. His eyes were frank, with a humorous expression in them, but though his face was lean there were deep lines from his nostrils to the corners of his mouth, and when he smiled, which he did easily, two more deep lines appeared in his cheeks.

Monroe was older, shorter, and stout. There was a smooth suavity in the effect of his neat, dapper person, his heavy gold watch chain, his eye glasses. He removed the glasses at intervals, as if from habit, wiping them with a silk handkerchief, and at such moments his blandly paternal manner was accentuated. His eyes were set too close to the thin bridge of a nose that grew heavy at the tip, but his gray hair, the kindly patronage of his smile, and his soft, heavy voice were impressive.

Rose perceived that both of these men were good salesmen, and that their working together made a happy combination of opposite abilities. She saw herself opposing them, an inexperienced girl, and felt that the odds were overwhelmingly against her. But her determination to fight was not lessened.

Upright on a hard red davenport, she argued. The territory was hers. She had come into it first. She had developed it. She conceded their right to work there, but not the justice of their demanding part of the commissions she earned. The stale little room, filled with smells of heat-blistered varnish and dusty plush, became a battleground, and the high back of the davenport was a wall against which she stood at bay, confronting these men who had come to rob her.

But she was a woman. They did not let her forget it. They asked her permission to smoke, but not her consent to their business arrangements. They smiled at her arguments. After all, she was of the sex that must be humored. "My dear Mrs. Lane," said Monroe, gallantly. "Do let us be reasonable." Their courtesy was perfect. They would let her talk, since it pleased her to do so. They would pick up her handkerchief when it slid from her lap. If it was her whim to work in the oil fields they would even indulge her in it. But she struck rock when she spoke of commissions. They would take two and a half percent from any sales she made.

It bored Hutchinson to point out the situation to her, but he did it, courteously. The firm had given them the territory. They were experienced salesmen. Naturally, Stine would not leave the territory in the hands of a young saleswoman, however charming personally. This was business, he gently explained. They would take two and a half percent.

But she was a woman, and a charming one. On sales they made from the leads she gave them, they would be generous. They would give her two and a half percent on those.

At this there was an interval when Rose sat smiling, speechless with rage. But she saw that the situation was hopeless. And every one of those names on her lists was a potential sale that would have paid her twelve and a half percent. Anger surged up in her, almost beyond her control. However, there was no value in fighting when she was beaten.

They parted on the best of terms; Rose yielded every point; she would give them the leads in the morning. She left them satisfied, thinking that women, while annoying, were not hard to handle.

In her room she stood shaken by her anger, by resentment and disgust. "Oh, beastly, beastly!" she said through clenched teeth. Striking her hand furiously against the edge of the dresser, she felt a physical pain that was a relief. She was able even to smile, ironically and wearily. This was the game she had to play, was it? Well, she would play it.

She sat down and from her notebook copied a list of names and addresses. She chose only those of men to whom she had talked until convinced they were not land buyers. In the morning she met Hutchinson in the lobby and gave him the list. She also insisted on a written agreement promising her two and a half per cent commission on sales made to any of those men. Hutchinson gave it to her in patronizing good humor.

Rose's buggy was waiting as usual in the shade of the hotel building. She felt grim satisfaction while she climbed into it and drove away toward the Limited lease. Hutchinson and Monroe would work industriously for some time before they perceived her duplicity, and she did not care about their opinion when they did discover it. Her own conscience was harder to handle, but she reflected that she would have to revise her standards of honesty.

She made another good sale before they stopped working on the worthless leads. Their attitude toward her changed abruptly.

"You certainly put one over on us," Hutchinson said without malice, and from that time they regarded her more as an equal than as a woman.

She was surprised to discover the bitterness developing in her.

Often in the evenings Rose walked in the quiet streets of little houses. Women were watering the lawns. A cool, sweet odor rose from refreshened grass and clumps of dripping flowers. Here and there a man leaned on the handle of a lawnmower, pipe in hand, talking to a neighbor. Children were playing in the twilight. Their young voices rose in happy shouts, and their feet pattered on the pavement. Hardness and bitterness vanished then, and Rose felt only an ache of wistfulness.

Later, lights shone through the deepening night, and the houses became dark masses framing squares of brightness. Vaguely beyond lace curtains Rose saw a woman swaying in a rocking chair, a group of girls gathered at a piano. From dim porches mothers called the children to bed, and at an upstairs window a shade came down like an eyelid. Rose felt alone and very lonely. She realized that she had been walking for a long time on tired feet. But she did not want to go back to the hotel. She must remind herself that tomorrow would be another hard day.

In the hotel lobby she encountered Hutchinson and Monroe. Sharpness and hardness came back then. Monroe was able to handle the smart young tool-dressers; his bland paternal manner crushed them into a paralyzing sense of their youth and crudeness. He had got hold of a tool-dresser she had canvassed and hoped to sell. That meant a fight about the commissions, in which, of course, Hutchinson backed Monroe. Rose was still alone, but now she was among enemies.

"You've got to fight!" she told herself. "Are you going to let them put it over on you because you're a woman?" She lay awake thinking of selling arguments, talking points, ways of handling this prospect and that. Every sale brought her nearer to freedom. Some day she would have a house, with a big gray living room, rose curtains, dozens of fine embroidered towels and tablecloths. She jerked her thoughts back to her work, angry at herself for letting them stray. But when, triumphantly, she closed the biggest sale yet, sixty acres! she celebrated by buying a linen lunch cloth stamped in a pattern of wild roses. She sat in her room in the evenings and embroidered it beautifully with fine even stitches.

When it was finished and laundered, she folded it in tissue-paper and put it carefully away in one of the cheap, warped drawers of her bureau. It lay in her thoughts like a nucleus of future contentment.

One day late in the fall Rose came in early from the oil fields. Over the level yellow plains a sense of autumn had come, an indefinable change in the air. She felt another change, too, a vague foreboding, something altered and restless in the spirit of the men with whom she had talked. For a week she had not found a new prospect, and two sales had slipped through her fingers. She stopped at the hotel to get a newspaper and read the financial news. Then she walked down Main Street to the little office Hutchinson and Monroe had rented.

Hutchinson was there, leaning back in a chair, his feet crossed on the desk. He did not move when she came in, save to lift his eyes from the sporting page and knock the ashes from his cigar. He accepted her now as an equal in his own game, and there was respect in his voice. "Well, how's it coming?"

"I'm going to get out of the fields," Rose said. She pushed back her hat with a tired gesture and dropped into a chair.

"The hell you say! What's wrong?" Hutchinson sat up, dropping the paper, and leaned forward on the desk. His interest was almost alarmed. She was making him money.

"The territory's gone bum. K.T.O. 25 will close down in another two weeks. The Limited's going to stop drilling. I'm going somewhere else."

"What! Who told you?"

"Nobody. I just doped it out."

He was relieved. He cajoled her. She was tired; she was working a streak of bad luck, he said. Every salesman struck it sometime. Look at him: he hadn't made a sale in four weeks, and he hadn't lost *his* nerve.

Rose had been considering a plan, and she had chosen the moment to present it to him. The obliqueness of real estate methods had astounded her. She had always sup-posed that men thought and acted in straight lines, logical lines. That, she had thought, gave them their superiority over irrational woman-kind. Her plan was logical, but she did not now, having altered that opinion, count upon its logic to impress Hutchinson. She reckoned on the emotional effect that would be produced by the truth of her prophecy. Letting it stand she began to unfold her plan.

The big point in making a land sale was getting a good prospect. That should not be done by personal canvassing. It was too wasteful of time and energy. It should be done by advertising. Now Stine & Kendrick's advertising was all "Whoop 'er up! Come on!" stuff. It made a bid for suckers. Hutchinson smiled, but she went on.

Men who would fall for that advertising were not of the class that had bank accounts. Hutchinson had lost a lot of money trying to sell the type of men who answered those advertisements. She mentioned cases, and Hutchinson's smile faded.

Rose proposed a new kind of real estate advertising; small type whose reading matter would be wholly sensible, straight-forward arguments. She was going into a settled farming community, where land values were high, and she was going to try out an advertising campaign for farmers. It had been a good farming year; farmers had money, and they had brains. She was going to offer them cheap land, and she was going to sell them.

Rose had the money to pay for the advertising, but she needed some one to work with her. She proposed that Hutchinson come in with her on a fifty-fifty basis. He could have his name on the door; he could make arrangements with the firm for the territory. They would hesitate to give it to her. But he knew she could sell land. Together they could make money.

Hutchinson did not take the proposition very seriously. She had not expected that he would. He thought about it, and grinned.

"I'd have to be mighty careful my wife didn't get wise!" he remarked.

"Cut that out!" Rose said in a voice that slashed. She unloosened her fury at him, at all men, and looked at him with blazing eyes. He stammered—he didn't mean—"When I talk business to you, don't forget that it's business," she said. She picked up her briefcase of maps and left the office. As she did so she reflected that the scheme would work out.

Ten days later word ran through the oil fields that all the K.T.O. leases were letting out men. Hutchinson's inquiries showed that the Limited was not starting any new wells. Monroe, who had saved his money, announced that he would stop work for the winter. Hutchinson, remembering that Mrs. Lane had funds for an advertising campaign, decided that her proposition offered a shelter in time of storm.

They talked it over again, considering the details, and Hutchinson went to the city to see Stine. He got a small advance on commission, and the Santa Clara Valley territory.

On the train, leaving the oil fields for the last time, Rose looked back at the little station, the sand hills covered with black derricks, the wide, level desert, and felt that she was leaving behind her the chrysalis of the woman she had become.

Part IV

Chapter 17

On a hot July afternoon three years later Rose Wilder Lane drove a dusty car through the traffic on Santa Clara Street in San Jose, and stopped it at the curb. She jumped to the sidewalk, walked around the car and thoughtfully kicked a balding tire with a stubby boot. It had gone flat on the Cupertino road and she thought she might have pumped too much air into the patched tube. For miles she had been expecting another blow-out but had been too weary to make the effort to stop and bleed air out.

"Darn thing's rim-cut, anyway," she said under her breath. "I'll have to get a new one." She dug her note book and wallet from the mass of dusty literature in the back seat and walked into the building.

Hutchinson was telephoning when she entered their office on the fourth floor. A curl of smoke rose from his cigar in the ashtray on the desk and drifted through the big open window. There were dusty footprints on the rug, and the helter-skelter position of the chairs showed that prospects had come in during her absence. Hutchinson chuckled when he hung up the receiver.

"Ted's going to catch it when he gets home!" he remarked, picking up the cigar.

"Cheating on his wife again?" Rose was running

through her mail. "Is there a man on earth who won't joyfully lie to another man's wife for him?" she added, ripping an envelope.

"Well, Holy Mike! What would you tell her?"

Rose looked up quickly from the letter.

"I'd tell her the truth!" she began hotly, and stopped. "Oh, I don't know. I suppose he's got that red-headed girl out in the car again? If you ask me, I think we'd better get rid of him. That sort of thing doesn't make us any sales."

There was silence while Rose ripped open the other letters and glanced through them. Her momentary anger subsided. She reflected that there were men on whom one could rely. Her thoughts returned to Paul as to a point of security. His appearance in San Jose a few months earlier had been like the sight of a cool spring in a desert. She had not realized the scorn for men that had grown in her until she met him again and could not feel it for him.

She glanced from the window at the clock in the tower of the Bank of San Jose building. Half-past four. He would still be at the ice plant. This thought, popping unexpectedly into her mind, startled her with the realization that all day she had been subconsciously dwelling on the fact that it was the day on which he usually came to San Jose since his firm had acquired its interests there.

The clock suggested simultaneously another thought, and she snatched the telephone receiver from its hook. "Am I too late for the afternoon delivery?" she asked the groceryman who answered the call. "Two heads of lettuce, a dozen eggs, half a pound of butter. How much are tomatoes? Well, send me a pound. Yes, R. W. Lane, 560 South Green Street. Thank you!" As the receiver clicked into place, she asked, "Any live ones today?"

"Six callers. Two good prospects and a couple that may work up into something," Hutchinson answered. "Say, the Seals are certainly handing it to the Tigers! Won in the fifth inning."

"That's good," she said absently. "Closed the Haas sale yet?"

"Oh, he's all right. Tied up solid." Hutchinson yawned. "How's your man?"

"Dated him for the land next Wednesday. He's live, but hard to handle. I'll drive him down."

"Car's all right?"

"Engine needs overhauling, and we've got to get a new rear tire and some tubes. Two blow-outs today. Time's too valuable to spend jacking up cars in this heat. I'm all in. But I can nurse the engine along till I get back from this trip." She felt that each sentence was a load she must lift with her voice. "I'm all in," she repeated. "Guess I'll call it a day."

However, Rose still sat relaxed in her chair, looking out at the quaint old red-brick buildings across the street. San Jose, she thought whimsically, was like a sturdy old geranium plant, woody-stemmed, whose roots were thick in every foot of the Santa Clara Valley. She felt an affection for the town, for the miles of orchard around it interlaced with trolley lines, for the thousands of bungalows on ranches no larger than gardens. Some day she would like to handle a subdivision of one-acre tracts, she thought, and build a hundred bungalows herself.

She brought her thoughts back to the Haas sale, and spoke of it tentatively. It was all right, Hutchinson assured her with some annoyance. Haas would sign the final contract as soon as he got his money, and he had written for it.

Where was Haas's money? Hutchinson replied that it was banked in the old country, Germany.

"Germany! And he's written for it? For the love of Mike! Good Lord, you grab the car and chase out there and make him cable. Pay for the cable and send it yourself. Tell his bank to cable the money over here. Haven't you seen the papers?"

Hutchinson, surrounded by scattered sporting sheets, stared up at her in amazement.

"Don't you know Austria sent an ultimatum to Serbia? Haven't you ever heard of the Balkan Wars? Don't you know if Russia—Good Lord, Hutchinson! And you're letting that money lie in Germany waiting for a letter? Beat it out there. A fifty-acre sale! Don't stop to talk. The cable office closes at six. Hurry!" Rose leaned out the door to call after him. "And look out for that left rear tire!"

The brief flurry of excitement had raised in her an exhilaration that vanished in a sense of futility and shame. "I'm getting so I swear like a land salesman!" Rose said to herself, straightening her hat before the mirror. A streak of dust on her nose: she wiped it off with a towel, and tucked up straggling locks of hair. In the dark strand over one temple a few white lines shone like silver. "I'm wearing out," she said, looking at them and at her skin, tanned to a smooth brown. Nobody cared. Why should she carefully save herself? She shut the closet door on her mirrored reflection, locked the office door, and went home.

The small, brown bungalow looked at Rose with empty eyes. The locked front door and the dry leaves scattered from the rose vines over the porch gave the place a deserted appearance. At all the other houses on the street the doors were open; children played on the lawns; wicker tables and rocking chairs and carelessly dropped magazines made the porches homelike. There was pity in her rush of affection for the little house; she felt toward it as she might have felt toward an animal she loved, waiting in loneliness for her coming to make it happy.

The door opened wide into the small square hall, and in the stirred air a few rose petals drifted downward from the bowl on the walnut table. She swung back the casement windows in the living room, dropped her hat and purse among the cushions on the window-seat, and straightening her body to its full height, relaxed again in a long, contented sigh. A weight slipped from her spirit. She was at home.

Her lingering glance caressed the rose-colored curtains rustling softly in the faint breeze, the cream walls, the brown rugs, the brick hearth on which piled logs waited for a match. There was her wicker sewing basket, and beyond it the crowded book shelves, the quaint walnut desk she had found at a second-hand store, and the big chair with brown leather cushions. It was all hers, her very own. She had made it. She was at home, and free. The silence around her was like cool water on a hot face.

In the white-tiled bathroom, with its yellow curtains, yellow bath rug, yellow-bordered fluffy bath towels, she washed the last memory of the office from her. She reveled in the daintiness of sheer, hand-embroidered underwear, in the crispness of the white dress she slipped over her head. She put on her feet the most frivolous of slippers, with beaded toes and high heels.

"You're a sybarite, that's what you are!" she laughed at herself in the mirror. "And you're leading a double life. 'Out, damned spot!' " she added, to the brown triangle of tan on her neck.

For an hour Rose was happy. Aproned in blue gingham she watered the lawn and hosed the last swirling leaf from the front porch. She said a word or two about roses to the woman next door. They were not very friendly; all the women on that street looked at her across the gulf of uncomprehension between quiet, homekeeping women and the vague world of business. They did not quite know how to take her; they thought her odd. She felt that their lives were cozy and safe, but very small.

Then Rose went into the kitchen. She made a salad, broke the eggs for an omelet, debated with finger at her lip whether to make popovers. They were fun to make, because of the uncertainty about their popping, but somehow they were difficult to eat while one read. One could manage bread-and-butter sandwiches without lifting eyes from the page. Odd, that she should be lonely only while she ate. The moment she laid down her book at the table the silence of the house closed around her coldly.

She would not have said that she was waiting for anything, but an obscure suspense prolonged her hesitation over the trivial question. When the telephone bell pealed startlingly through the stillness it was like an awaited summons, and she ran to answer it without doubting whose voice she would hear.

As always, there was some excuse for Paul's telephoning: a message from his mother, a bit of news from Ripley Farmland Acres, some negligible matter which she heard without listening, knowing that to both of them it was unimportant. The nickel mouthpiece reflected an amused dimple in her cheek, and there was a lilt in her voice when she asked him to come to supper. His hesitation was a struggle with longing. She insisted, and when she hung up the receiver the house had suddenly become warmed and glowing.

Rose felt a new zest while she took her prettiest lunch cloth from its lavender-scented drawer and brought in a bunch of roses, stopping to tuck one in her belt. She felt that she was pushing back into the depths of her mind many thoughts and emotions that struggled to emerge. She shut her eyes to them, and resisted blindly. It was better to see only the placid surface of the moment. She concentrated her attention on the popovers, and the egg beater was humming in her hands when she heard his step on the porch.

It was a quick, masculine and determined step, but always there was something boyishly eager in it.

Rose called to him through the open doors, and when he came in she gave him a floury hand, pushing a lock of hair from her eyes with the back of it before she went on beating the popovers. He stood awkwardly about while she poured the mixture into the hot tins and quickly slid it into the oven, but she knew he enjoyed being there.

The table was set on the screened side porch. White passion flowers fluttered like moths among the green leaves that curtained it, and in an open space a great, yellow rose tapped gently against the screen. The twilight was filled with a soft, orange flow; above the gray roofs half the sky was yellow and the small clouds were like flakes of shining gold.

There came over Rose the strange, uncanny sensation that sometime, somewhere, she had lived through this moment once before. She ignored it, smiling across the white cloth at Paul. She liked to see him sitting there, his square shoulders in the gray business suit, his lips firm, tight at the corners, his eyes a little stern, but straight-forward and honest. He gave an impression of solidity and permanence; one would always know where to find him.

"You surely are some cook, Rose!" he said. The omelet was delicious, and the popovers a triumph. She ate only one, that he might have the others, and his enjoyment of them gave her a deep delight.

Across the little table a subtle current vibrated between them, intoxicating her, making her a little dizzy with emotions she would not analyze.

"I certainly am!" she laughed. "The dinner table lost a genius when I became a real estate lady." She was not blind to the shadow that crossed his face, but part of her intoxication was a perverseness that did not mind annoy-ing him just a bit.

"I hate to think about it," Paul said. His gravity shattered the iridescent glamor, making her grave, too, and the prosaic atmosphere of the office and its problems surrounded her.

"Well, you may not have it to think about much longer.

What do you think? Is there going to be real trouble in Europe?"

"How do you mean?"

"War?"

"Oh, I doubt it. Not in this day and age. We've got beyond that, I hope." His casual dismissal of the possibility was a relief to her, but not quite an assurance.

"I certainly hope so." Rose stirred her coffee, thoughtfully watching the glimmer of the spoon in the golden-brown depths. "But if Austria stands by her ultimatum, and Serbia does pull Russia into it, there's Germany. I don't know much about world politics, but one thing's certain. If there is war, the bottom'll drop out of my business."

He was startled.

"I don't know what it's got to do with us over here."

"It hasn't anything to do with you or your affairs. But farmers are the most cautious people on earth. The minute there is a real storm cloud in Europe nearly every one of them will draw in his money and sit on it. The land game's entirely a matter of psychology. Let the papers begin yelling, 'War!' and though it's eight thousand miles away, practically every prospect I have will figure that good hard cash in hand is better than a mortgage with him on the wrong side of it. That means thumbs down for me. It's hard enough to cover office expenses and pay garage bills as it is."

Alarm was driven from his face by a chaos of emotions. He flushed darkly, his eyes on his plate. "You oughtn't to have to worry about such things." Rose's words forestalled him, still pleasantly commonplace.

"It's getting dark, isn't it? Let's go in and light the lamps."

His footsteps followed her through the ghostly dimness of the house. The floor seemed far beneath Rose's feet, and through her quivering emotions shot a gleam of amusement. She was feeling like a girl in her teens. Her hand sought the light switch as it might have clutched at a life-line.

"Rose, wait a minute!" She started, stopped, her arm outstretched toward the wall. "I've got to say something."

The tortured determination of his voice told her that the coming moment could not be evaded. A cool, accustomed steadiness of nerves and brain rose to meet it. She crossed the room, and switched on the tiny desk lamp, the golden-shaded light of which only warmed the dusk. But her opened lips made no sound; she indicated the big, leather chair only with a gesture, settling herself on the cushioned window-seat. Paul remained standing, his hands in his coat pockets, his gaze on the fingers interlaced on her knees.

"You're a married woman."

A shock ran through her. She had worn those old bonds so long without feeling them that she had forgotten they were there. She was herself, R. W. Lane, salesman, office-manager, householder.

His voice went on stubbornly, hoarse.

"I haven't got any right to talk this way. But, Rose, what are you going to do? Don't you see I've got to know? Don't you see I can't go on? It isn't fair." He faltered, dragging out the words as though by muscular effort. "It isn't fair to me or you, or . . . him, Rose. If things do go to pieces, as you said, can't you see I'll have to be in a position to *do* something?"

The tremulous intoxication was gone. Her composed self-possession of the moment before seemed a cheap, smug attitude. She saw a naked, tortured soul, and the stillness of the room was reflected in the stillness within her.

"What do you want me to do?" she said at last.

He walked to the cold hearth and stood looking down at the piled logs. His voice, coming from the shadows, sounded as though muffled by them. "Do you still care about him?"

All the wasted love and broken hopes, the muddled, miserable tangle of living, swept over her. The suffering that had been buried by many days, the memories she had locked away and smothered, Gil, and all that he had been to her. And now she could not remember his face. She could not see him clearly in her mind; she did not know where he was. When had she thought of him last?

"No," she said.

"Then, can't you?"

"Divorce, you mean?"

Paul came back to her, and she saw that he was even more shaken than she. He spoke thickly, painfully. He had never thought that he would do such a thing. God knew, he said without irreverence, that he did not believe in divorce. Not usually. But in this case . . . He had never thought he could love another man's wife. He had tried not to. But she was so alone. And he had loved her long ago. She had not forgotten that? It hadn't been easy to keep on all these years without her. And then when she had been treated so, and he couldn't do anything.

But it wasn't altogether that. Not all unselfish. "I've wanted you so! You don't know how I've wanted you. Nobody ever seems to think that a man wants to be loved and have somebody caring just about him, somebody that's glad when he comes home, and cares when he's blue. We aren't supposed to feel like that. But we do; I do terribly. Not just 'somebody.' It's always been you I wanted. Nobody else. Oh, there were girls. I even tried to think that maybe—but somehow, none of them were you. I couldn't help coming back."

"Oh, my dear, my dear!" Rose said, with tears on her cheeks.

Perhaps, after all, forgetting the past and the things that

had been between them, they could come together again and be happy. The tragedy that shook her was that all the passion and beauty of her old love for Gil was dead, lying like a corpse in her heart, never to be awakened and never utterly forgotten.

"I will be free," she promised, knowing that she never would be. But in her deepest tenderness toward Paul she could shut her eyes to that. The promise made him happy. Despite his doubts, his restless conscience not quite silenced, he was happy, and his happiness was reflected in her. Something of magic revived, making the moment glamorous. She need not think of the future; she need make no promises beyond that one.

For the moment her tenderness enfolded him, who loved her so much that she could never give him enough to repay him. It came to her in a clear flash of thought through one of their silences that the maternal quality in a woman's love is not so much due to the mother in the woman as to the child in the man.

"Dearest," she said.

He had to go at last, but he would write her every day. "And you'll see about it right away?"

"Yes, right away." The leaves of the rose vines over the porch rustled softly; a scented petal floated down through the moonlight. "Goodnight, dear."

"Goodnight." He hesitated, holding her hand. Then, quickly, he went.

Rose entered a house filled with silence that turned to her many faces, and switching off the lamp she sat a long time in the darkness, looking out at the moonlit lawn. She was tired. It was good to be alone in the stillness, not to think, but to feel herself slowly growing composed again around a quietly happy heart.

Something of the glow went with her to the office next morning and stayed with her all day while she talked subsoils, water depths, prices, terms, while she answered her letters, wrote next week's advertising, corrected proofs. The news in the papers was disquieting; it appeared that the cloud over Europe was growing blacker. How long would it be if war did come before its effect reached her territory, slowly cut off her sales? Ted Collins' bill for gasoline was out of all reason; there was a heated discussion in the office, telephone messages to Stine in San Francisco. Business details engulfed her.

On Wednesday Rose took her difficult prospect to the Sacramento lands. He was hard to handle; salesmen for other tracts had clouded the clear issue. She fell back on the old expedient of showing him all those other tracts herself, with a fair-seeming impartiality that damned them by indirection. There was no time for dreaming during those hard three days: toiling over dusty fields with a soil-augur, skillfully countering objections before they took form, nursing an engine that coughed on three cylinders, dragging the man at last by sheer force of will power to the point of signing on the dotted line. She came exhausted into the Sacramento hotel late the third night, with no thought in her mind but a bath and bed.

Stopping at the telegraph counter to wire the firm that the sale was closed, she heard a familiar voice at her elbow, and turned.

"Mr. Monroe! You're up here too! How's it going?" She gave him a dust-grimed hand.

"Well, I'm not complaining, Mrs. Lane, not complaining. Just closed thirty-five acres. And how are you? Fortune smiling, I hope?"

"Just got in from the tract. Sold a couple of twenty-acre pieces."

"Is that so? Fine work, fine work! Keep it up. It's a pleasure to see a young lady doing so well. Well, well, and so you've been out on the tract! I wonder if you've seen

Gillette yet?" His shrewd old gossip-loving eyes were upon her. She turned to her message on the counter, and after a pause of gazing blindly at it, she scrawled, "R. W. Lane," clearly below it. "Send it collect," she said to the girl, and over her shoulder, "Gillette who? Not my husband?"

Yes, Monroe had run across him in San Francisco, and he was looking well, very well indeed. He had asked about her; Monroe had told him she was in San Jose. "But if you were on the tract, no doubt he failed to find you?"

"Yes," she said. "I've been lost to the world for three days. Showed my prospect every inch of land between here and Patterson. You know how it is. I'm all in. Well, goodbye. Good luck." As she crossed the lobby to the elevator she heard her heels clicking on the mosaic floor, and knew she was walking with her usual quick, firm step.

Chapter 18

Sleep would be impossible. Rose's exhausted nerves reacted in feverish tenseness to the shock of this unexpected news of Gil. From long experience she knew that in this half-delirious state she could not trust her reasoning, must not accept seriously its conclusions, but she could not stop her thoughts from running uncontrolled through her brain as if driven by a life of their own. She could only endure them until her overtaxed body crushed them with its tired weight. Tomorrow she would be able to think.

In the square hotel room, under the garish light that emphasized the ugliness of red carpet and varnished mahogany furniture, she moved about as usual, opening the windows, hanging up her hat and coat, unfastening her bag. She did not forget the customary pleasant word to the bell-boy who brought ice water, and he saw nothing unusual in her white face and bright eyes. This hotel saw her only on her return trips from the tract, and she was always exhausted after making or losing a sale. She locked the door behind him, and began to undress.

Paul must not be involved. She must manage to shield him. A sensation of nausea swept over her. The vulgarity, the cheap coarseness of it! But she must not think. She was too tired. Why had she blundered into such a situation?

What change had the years made in Gil? Her thoughts, touching him, recoiled. She would not think of Paul. To have the two in her mind together was intolerable; it was the essence of her humiliation. Married to one man, bound to him by a thousand memories that rushed upon her, and loving another, engaged to him! No fine, self-respecting woman could be in such a position. But she was. She must face that fact. No, she must not face it. Not until she was rested, in command of herself.

She bathed, scrubbing her skin until it glowed painfully. Cold-cream was not enough for her face and hands. She rubbed them with soap, with harsh towels. At midnight she was washing her hair. If only she could slip out of her body, run away from herself into a new personality, forget completely all that she was or had been!

This was hysteria, she told herself. "Only hold on, have patience, wait. The days will go past you. Life clears itself, like running water. It will be all right somehow. Don't try to think. You're too tired."

At dawn her eyelids were weary at last, and she fell asleep. She prolonged the sleep consciously, half waking at intervals as the day grew brighter, pulling oblivion over her head again to shield herself from living, as a child hides beneath a quilt to keep away darkness.

Outside the world had awakened, going busily about its affairs while the day passed over it. The noise of the streets, voices, automobile horns, rumbling wheels, came through the open windows with the hot sunshine, running like the sound of a river through her sleep. She awoke in the late afternoon, heavy-lidded, with creased cheeks, but once more quietly self-controlled.

Refreshed by a cold plunge, crisply dressed, composed, Rose ate dinner in the big, softly lighted dining room, nodding across white tables to the business men she knew. Then, led by an impulse she did not question, she went out into the crowded streets. With her walked the ghost of the girl who had come from Mansfield, dazzled, wide-eyed, so pitifully sure of herself, to learn to telegraph.

Sacramento had changed. It had been a big town; it was now a city, radiating interurban lines, thrusting tall buildings toward the sky, smudging that sky with the smoke of factories and canneries. Its streets were sluggishly moving floods of automobiles; its wharves were crowded with boats; across the wide, yellow river spans of new bridges were reaching toward each other.

All the statistics of the city's growth, of the great reclamation projects, of the rich farms spreading over the old grain lands, were at Rose's fingertips. A hundred times she had gone over them, drawn conclusions from them, pounded home-selling arguments with them since she had added Sacramento valley lands to the San Joaquin properties she handled. But more eloquently her reviving memories showed her the gulf between the old days and the new.

Mrs. Brown's little restaurant and the room where Rose had lived, were gone. In their place stood a six-story office building of raw new brick. That imposing street down which she had stumbled awkwardly after Mrs. Campbell was now a row of dingy boarding-houses. Mrs. Campbell's house itself, once so awe-inspiring, had become a disconsolate building with peeling paint, standing in a ragged lawn, and across the porch where she and Paul had said goodbye in the dawn there was now a black and gold sign, "Ah Wong, Chinese Herb Doctor." She went quickly past it.

For the first time in the hurried years Rose's thoughts turned inward, self-questioning, and she tried to follow step by step the changes that had taken place in her. But she could not see them clearly for the memory of the girl that she had been, a girl she saw now as a piteous young thing quite outside herself, a lovely, emotional, valiant young struggler against unknown odds. She felt an aching compassion, a longing to shield that girl from the life she had faced with such blind courage, to save her youth and sweetness. But the girl, of course, was gone, like the room from which she had looked so eagerly at the automobile.

It was eleven o'clock when she walked briskly through the groups in the hotel lobby, took her key from the room clerk and left a call for the early San Francisco train. She would reach the city in time to get the final contracts for the sale she had made yesterday, to take them to San Jose and get them signed the same day. The thought of Gil lay like a menace in the back of her mind, but she kept it there. She could not foresee what would happen; she would meet it when it occurred. Meantime she would go about her work as usual. Her attitude toward the future, her attitude toward even herself, was one of waiting. She fell quietly asleep.

On the train next morning she bought the San Francisco papers. The headlines screamed the news at her. It was war. The news had made no change in the atmosphere of Stine & Kendrick's wide, clean-looking office, where salesmen lounged against the counters, their elbows resting on plate glass that covered surveyor's maps and photographs of alfalfa fields. The talk, as she stopped to speak to one and another, was the usual news of sales made and lost, quarrels over commissions, personal gossip. She waited her turn to enter Mr. Stine's office, and when it came she looked at him with a keenness hidden under the friendliness of her eyes.

She liked to talk to Mr. Stine. Three years of working with him had brought her an understanding of this nervous, quick-witted, harassed man. There was comradeship between them, a sympathy tempered by wariness on both sides. Neither would have lost the slightest business advantage for the other, but beyond that necessary antagonism they were friends. She watched with pleasure the quick play of his mind, managing hers as he would have handled the thoughts of a buyer; she was conscious that he saw the motives behind her method of counter-attack; a business interview between them was like a friendly bout between fencers. But Mr. Stine spoke to her sometimes of the wife and children whose pictures were on his desk; she knew how deeply he was devoted to them. And once, during an idle evening in a Stockton hotel, he had held her breathless with the whole story of his business career, talking to her as he might have talked to himself.

Today there seemed to her an added shade of effort in his briskly cheerful manner. The lines around his shrewd eyes had deepened since she first knew him, and it struck her, as she settled into the chair facing his across the flat desk, that his hair was quite gray. With the alert, keen expression taken from his face he would appear an old man.

This expression was intensified when she spoke of the war, questioned its effect on the business. It would have no effect, he assured her. The future had never been brighter; Sacramento lands were booming; fifty new settlers were going into Ripley Farmland Acres that fall. Chaos on the stock market would make the solid investment values of land even more apparent. If the war lasted a year or longer the prices of American crops would rise.

"I was wondering about the psychological effect," she murmured. Mr. Stine ran a nervous hand through his hair.

"High prices will take care of the buyer's psychology."

Rose laughed. "While you take care of the salesman's." A twinkle in his eyes answered the smile in hers, but she spoke again before he replied. "Mr. Stine, I'd like to ask you something rather personal. What do you really get out of business?"

A smile deepened the lines around his mouth. "Well, I got nearly one million dollars out of it in the Portland boom. It's a game," he said, "just a game to me. That's all.

I've made two fortunes (you know that) and lost them. And now I'm climbing up again. Oh, if I had my life to start over again, I . . ." He changed the words on his lips, "I'd do the same thing. No doubt about it. We all think we wouldn't, but we would. We don't make our lives. They make us."

"Fatalist?"

"Fatalist." They smiled at each other again as she rose and held out her hand. He kept it a moment in a steadying grasp. "By the way, have you heard that your husband's around?"

"Yes." She thanked him with her eyes. "Goodbye."

Rose was oppressed by a sense of futility, of the hopeless muddle of living, while the train carried her down the peninsula toward San Jose. To escape from it she concentrated her attention on the afternoon papers.

They were filled with wild rumors, with names of strange towns in Belgium, a mass of clamoring bulletins, confusing, yet somehow making clear a picture of gray hordes moving, irresistible as a monstrous machine, toward France, toward Paris. Intolerable, that the Germans should march into Paris! She was surprised by her passion of resistance. Why should she care so fiercely, she who knew nothing of Paris, nothing of Germany, nothing but chance scraps of facts about Europe?

"I must learn French," Rose said to herself, and was appalled by the multitude of things she did not know, both without and within herself.

The unsigned contracts in their long manila envelope were like an anchor in a tossing sea. She must get them signed that night. It was something to do, a definite action. She telephoned from the station, making an appointment with the buyer, and felt the familiar routine closing around her again while the streetcar carried her down First Street to her office.

Gil was sitting in her chair, smoking and talking

enthusiastically to Hutchinson, when she opened the door. The shock petrified them all. The two men stared at her, Hutchinson's expression of easy good humor frozen on his face; Gil's hand, extended in the old, flashing gesture, suspended in the air. The door closed behind her.

Later she remembered Hutchinson's blood-red face, his awkward, even comical efforts to stammer that he hadn't expected her, that he must be going, his blind search for his hat, his confused departure. At the moment she seemed to be advancing to meet Gil in an otherwise empty room, and though she felt herself trembling from head to foot her hands and her voice were quite steady.

"How do you do?" Rose said, beginning to unbutton her gloves.

Though she had not been able to remember his face, it was as familiar as if she had seen it every day; the low white forehead with the lock of fair hair across it, the bright eyes, the aquiline nose, the rather shapeless mouth. Rose had not remembered that his mouth was like that. Her experienced eye saw self-indulgence and dissipation in the soft flesh of his cheeks, the faint puffiness of the eyelids. Her trembling was increasing, but it did not affect her. She was quite cool and controlled.

She heard unmoved his cajoling, confident expostulation. That was a nice way to meet a man when he'd come— she brushed aside his embracing arm with a movement of her shoulder. "We'd better sit down. Pardon me." She took the chair he had left, her own chair, from which she had handled so many land buyers.

"God, but you're hard!" Gil's accusation held an unwilling admiration. She saw that the way to lose this man was to cling to him; he wanted her now, because she had no need of him. Memories of all the wasted love, the self-surrender and faith she had given him, for which he had not cared at all, which he had never seen or known how to value, came back to her in a flood of pain. Rose's lips tightened, and looking at him across the desk, she said:

"Do you think so? I'm sorry. What do you want?"

He met her eyes for a moment, and she saw his effort to adjust himself, his falling back upon his old self-confidence in bending other minds to his desires. He could not believe that anyone would successfully resist him, that any woman was impervious to his charm. And suddenly she felt hard, hard through and through. She wanted to hurt him cruelly; she wanted to tear and wound his self-centered egotism, to reach somewhere a sensitive spot in him and stab it.

He wanted her, Gil said. He wanted his wife. She heard in his voice a note she knew, the deep, caressing tone he kept for women, and she understood that he used it skillfully, aware of its effect.

He had gone through hell. "Through *hell*," he repeated vibrantly. He did not expect her to understand. She was a woman. She could not realize the tortures of remorse, the agonies of soul, the miseries of those years without her. He sketched them for her, with voice and gestures appealing to her pity. He had been a brute to her; he had been a yellow cur to leave her so. He admitted it, magnificently humble.

He had promised himself that he would not come back to her until he was on his feet again. He had reformed. He was going to work. He was going to cut out the booze. Already he had the most glittering prospects. Fer de Leon, the king of patent-medicine men, was going to put on a tremendous campaign in Australia. Fer de Leon had absolute confidence in him; he could sign a contract at any time for fifteen thousand a year.

He wanted her to come with him. He needed her. With her beside him he could resist all temptations. She was an angel; she was the only woman he had ever really loved and respected. With her he could do anything. Without her he would be hopeless, heartsick. God only knew what would happen. "You'll forgive me, won't you? You won't turn me down. You'll give me another chance?"

Rose was looking down at her hands, unable any longer to read what her eyes saw in him. Her hands lay folded on the edge of the desk, composed and quiet, not moved at all by the sick trembling that was shaking her. The desire to hurt him was gone. His appeal to her pity had dissolved it in contempt.

"I'm sorry," she said with effort. "I hope you will go on and succeed in everything. I know you will, of course." She said it in a tone of strong conviction, trying now to save his ego. She did not want to hurt him. "I know you have done the best you could. It's all right. It isn't anything you've done. I don't blame you for that. But it seems to me . . ."

"Good God! How can you be so cold?" Gil cried.

Even her hands were shaking now, and Rose quieted them by clasping them together. "Perhaps I am cold," she said. "We didn't make a success of it. It isn't your fault. We just don't suit each other. It was all a mistake." Her throat contracted.

"So it's another man!" he said. "I might have known it."

"No." She was quiet even under the sneer. "It isn't that. But there was never anything to build on between you and me. You think you want me now only because you can't have me. So it will not really hurt you if I get a divorce. And I'd rather do that. Then we can both start again with clean slates. And I hope you will succeed. And have everything you want." She rose, one hand heavily on the desk, and held out the other. "Goodbye."

Rose's attempt to end the scene with frankness and dignity failed. Gil could not believe that he had lost this object he had attempted to gain. His wounded vanity demanded that he conquer her resistance. He recalled their memories of happiness, tried to sway her with pictures of the future he would give her, appealed to generosity, to pity, to admiration. He played upon every chord of the feminine heart that he knew.

She stood immovable, sick with misery, and saw behind his words the motives that prompted them; self-love, self-assurance, baffled antagonism. She felt again, as something outside herself, the magnetism, the force like an electric current, that had conquered her once.

"I really wish you would go," she said. "All this gains nothing for either of us."

At last he went.

"You women are all alike. Don't think you've fooled me. It's another man with more money. If I weren't a gentleman you wouldn't get away so easily with this divorce talk. But I am. Go get it!" The door crashed behind him.

Rose did not move for a long moment. Then she went into the inner office, locked the door behind her, and sat down. Her glance fell on her clenched hands. She had not worn her wedding ring for some time, but the finger was still narrowed a little, and on the inner side a smooth, white mark showed where it had been. Quietly she folded her arms on the desk and hid her face against them. After a little while she began to sob, rough, hard sobs that tore her throat and forced a few burning tears from her eyes.

An hour went by. She was roused by the familiar noise of the streets: streetcars clanged past, a newsboy cried an extra. Across the corner the hands of the clock in the Bank of San Jose building marked off the minutes with little jerks.

It was six o'clock. An urgent summons knocked at a closed door in her mind. Six o'clock. She looked at her wrist watch, and memory awoke. She had an appointment at six-thirty to close the final contracts on the forty-acre sale. Below the window the newsboy cried "War!" again.

Wearily Rose bathed her face with cold water, combed her hair, adjusted her hat. Contracts in hand, she locked the office door behind her, and her face wore its necessary pleasant, untroubled expression. The buyer's wife was charmed by her smile, and although the man was already somewhat disturbed by the war news, Rose was able to persuade them to sign the contracts.

A week later Rose announced to Hutchinson that she was going to stop selling land. She could give him no reasons that satisfied his startled curiosity. She was simply quitting; that was all. He could manage the office himself or get another partner; her leaving would make little difference.

He protested, trying half-heartedly to shake her determination. The shattering of accustomed and pleasant routine shocked him; he was like a person thrown suddenly from a boat into unstable water.

"Why? What's the idea? Aren't we getting along all right?" He was longing to ask if she were going to Gil, whose arrival and immediate departure had not been explained to him. The whole Stine & Kendrick organization, she knew, was discussing it, and Hutchinson, on the very scene of their meeting, was in the unhappy position of being unable to give the interesting details. But he did not quite venture to break through her reserve with a direct question.

He scouted her suggestion that the war would affect business. "Why, things have never looked better! Here we've just made a forty-acre sale. Sacramento's booming, and so is the San Joaquin. Fifty new settlers are going into Farmland Acres this fall. There's going to be a boom in land. Folks are going to see what a solid investment it is, the way stocks are tumbling. And the farmers are going to make money hand over fist if the war lasts a couple of years."

"Maybe you're right," she conceded, remembering the twinkle in Mr. Stine's eye when she had accused him of taking care of the salesman's psychology. She believed that spring would see a slump in real estate business. She had learned too well that men did not handle their affairs on a basis of cool logic; too often in her own work she had taken advantage of the gusts of impulse and unreasoning emotion that swayed them. There would be a period when they would be afraid; no facts or arguments would persuade them to exchange solid cash for heavily mortgaged land. But that point no longer interested her.

Rose felt a profound weariness, an unease of spirit that was like the ache of a body too long held motionless. Business had rested on her like a weight for nearly four years. She could bear it no longer. She must relax the self-control that held her own impulses and emotions in its tight grip. The need was too strong to be longer resisted, too deep in herself to be clearly understood. "I'm tired," she said. "I'm going to quit."

An agreement dividing their deferred commissions must be drawn up and filed with the San Francisco office. Hutchinson took over her half-interest in the automobile she had left to be repaired in Sacramento. Already his mind was busy with new plans. Since she would no longer write the advertising he would cut it out. "Want ads'll be cheaper and good enough," he said.

Thus simply the bonds were cut between her and all that had filled her days and thoughts. Rose went home to the little bungalow, hung her hat and coat in the closet.

The house seemed strange, with early-afternoon sunlight streaming through the living room windows. It was delightfully silent and empty. Long hours, weeks, months, stretched before her like blank pages on which she might write anything she chose.

She went through the rooms, straightening a picture, moving a chair, taking up a vase of withering flowers. The curtains stirred in a cool breeze that poured through the open windows and ruffled her hair. It seemed to blow through her thoughts, too; she felt clean and cool and refreshed. With a deep, simple joy she began to think of little things. She would discharge the woman who came to clean; she would polish the windows and dust the furniture and wash the dishes herself. Tomorrow she would get gingham and make aprons. Perhaps her mother and father would come for a visit; she would write and ask them.

She was cutting roses to fill the emptied vase when she thought of Paul. He came into her thoughts quite simply, as he had come before Gil's return. She thought, with a warmth at her heart and a dimple in her cheek, that she would telephone him to come next Sunday, and she would make a peach shortcake for him.

Chapter 19

The shortcake was a triumph when she set it, steaming hot and oozing amber juice, on the table between them. "You certainly are a wonder, Rose!" Paul said, struck by its crumbling perfection. "We haven't been in the house an hour, and with a simple twist of the wrist you produce a dinner like this! Lucky we aren't living a couple of centuries ago: you'd been burned for a witch." His eyes, resting on her, were filled with warm light.

Already he seemed to radiate a glow of contentment; the hint of sternness in his face had melted in a joy that was almost boyish, and all day there had been a touch of possessive pride in his contemplation. It intoxicated her; she felt the exhilaration of victory in her submission to it, and a sense of power over him gave sparkle to her delight in his nearness.

Rose's bubbling spirits had been irrepressible; she had flashed into whimsicalities, laughed at him, teased him, melted into sudden tendernesses. Together they had played with light-hearted absurdities, chattering nonsense while they explored a rocky canyon in Alum Rock Park, a canyon peopled only with bright-eyed furtive creatures of the forest whisking through tangled underbrush and over fallen logs. They had looked at each other with dancing eyes, smothering bursts of mirth like children hiding some riotous joke when they came down into the holiday crowd around the hot dog counters at the park gate and had bought ice-cream cones from a vendor near a hurdy-gurdy.

Now she looked at him across her own dinner table, and felt that the last touch of perfection had been given a happy day. She laughed delightedly.

"It's a funny thing when you think of it," he went on, pouring cream over the fruity slices. "You're working all week in an office—just about as good a little business woman as they make 'em, I guess—and then on top of it you come home and cook like mother never did. It beats me."

"Well, I like to cook," Rose said. "It's recreation. Lots of successful business men are pretty good golf players. Besides I'm not a business woman any more. I've left the office. Shall I pour your coffee now?"

"Left the office!" he exclaimed. "What for? When?"

"The other day. Why, Paul?" She was startled by his expression.

"Well, you didn't give me any idea ..." There was a shade of reproach in his tone, which shifted quickly to pugnacity. "That partner of yours. He hasn't been putting anything over on you?"

"Why, no, of course not! I just made up my mind to stop selling land. I'm tired of it. Besides, it looks as though there'll be a slump in the business."

"Well, you can't tell. However, you may be right," he conceded.

As she dropped the sugar into his coffee cup and tilted the percolator, a memory flashed across her mind. She saw him sitting at a little table in a dairy lunch room, struggling to hide his embarrassment, carefully dipping two spoonsful of sugar from the chipped white bowl, and the memory brought with it many others.

The iridescent mood of the afternoon was gone, and

reaching for the deeper and more firm basis of emotion between them, she braced herself to speak of another thing she had not told him.

Constraint had fallen upon them; they were separated by their diverging thoughts, and uneasily, with effort, they broke the silence with disconnected scraps of talk. Time was going by; already twilight crept into the room, and looking at his watch, Paul spoke of his train. Rose led the way to the porch, where the shade of climbing rose vines softened the last clear gray light of the day. There was sadness in this wan reflection of the departed sunlight; the air was still, and the creaking of the wicker chair, when Rose settled into it, the sharp crackle of Paul's match as he lighted his after-dinner cigar, seemed irreverently loud. With a sudden keen need to be nearer to him, Rose drew a deep breath, preparing to speak and to clear away forever the last barrier between them.

But his words met hers before they were uttered.

"What are you going to do, then, Rose? Unless you are going home to Mansfield?" he added, before her uncom-prehension.

"Well, I haven't thought, exactly. I'd like to stay here in my own house. There's so much to do in a house," she said, vaguely. "I've never had time to do it before."

Paul's voice was indulgent.

"That'll be fine! It's just what you ought to have a chance to do. But, Rose, of course it's none of my business yet, in a way, but naturally I'll worry about it. It takes an income to keep up a house; and I'd like you to know that everything I've got is just the same as yours, already."

"Paul, you're a dear! Don't worry about that at all. If I need any help I'll ask you, truly. But I won't."

"Well, we might as well look at it practically," he persisted. "It may amount to more than you've figured to keep this house going. Not that I want you to give it up if you'd rather stay here," he added quickly. "I'd rather have you here than in Mansfield. But I'd rather have you in Ripley than here, for that matter. Why couldn't you come down there? I could fix up that little bungalow on Harper Street. And everyone knows that you're an old friend of mother's."

"I might do something like that," Rose said at random. She was troubled by the knowledge that their hour was slipping past and the conversation going in the wrong direction.

"It would cost you hardly anything to live there. And we could see each other a lot!"

"Yes," Rose said. "I'd love that part of it. You know how I'd like to see you every minute. But there's plenty of time. I'll think about it, dear."

"That's just the point. There is so much time. A whole year and more, and it would be just like you to half starve yourself and never say a word to me about it."

"Oh, Paul!" she laughed, "you are so funny! And I love you for it. Well, then, listen. I have a little over twelve hundred dollars in the bank. Not much, is it, to show for the years I've been working? But it will keep me from growing gaunt and hollow-eyed for lack of food for quite a little while. And if I really did need more there's a whole world full of money all around me, you know. So please don't worry: I promise to eat and eat. I promise never to stop eating as long as I live. Regularly, three times a day, every single day!"

"All right," Paul said. His cigar-end glowed red for a minute through the gathering dusk. She put her hand on his arm, and the muscles moved beneath her fingers. Then his firm, warm grip closed over them. Palm against palm and fingers interlaced, they sat in silence. "It's going to be a long time," he said. After a long moment he added gruffly, "I suppose you've seen a lawyer?"

"I'm going to this week."

"You poor dear! I wish you didn't have to go through it. But I suppose there won't be any trouble. Tell me, Rose, honestly. You do want to do it?"

"Yes, I do want to. But there's something I've got to tell you. Gil's come back." Paul was instantly so still that his immobility was more startling than a cry. At the faint relaxing of his hand, Rose's fled, and clenched on the arm of her chair. Quietly, in a voice that was stiff from being held steady, she told him something of her interview with Gil. "I thought you ought to know. I didn't want you to hear it from someone else."

"I'm glad you told me. But don't let's ever speak of him again." His gesture of repugnance flung the cigar in a glowing arc over the porch railing, and it lay a red coal in the grass.

"I don't want to." Rose stood up to face him, putting her hands on his shoulders. "But, Paul, I want you to understand. He never was real to me. It was just because I was a foolish girl and lonely and tired of working, and I didn't understand. We never were really *married.*" She stumbled among inadequate words, trying to make him feel what she felt. "There wasn't any reality between us, any real love, nothing solid to build a marriage on. And I think there is between you and me."

"The only thing I want," Paul said, his arms around her, "the only thing I want in the world is just to take you home and take care of you."

She kissed him, a hushed solemnity in her heart. He was so good, so fine and strong. With all her soul she longed to be worthy of him, to make him happy, to be able to build with him a serene and beautiful life.

Epilogue

Rose didn't marry Paul.

While waiting for her divorce from Gillette to become effective, Rose became restless; she couldn't settle down to an unchallenging, uneventful existence in her beloved house. She conceived the idea of a promotional scheme based on her years as a business woman and took it to a California publication. They were intrigued by Rose's perception and clarity of description, although not by the scheme. Rose began to write for them and—as her interest in writing grew—gravitated back to San Francisco—the West's literary mecca. She came to the notice of Bessie Beatty, who was then women's editor of the San Francisco *Examiner,* and of Fremont Older, its famous editor. The two of them taught Rose how really to write, and she was on her way as one of the paper's most popular writers. In a couple of years she was herself one of the celebrities of San Francisco.

Though she continued to see Paul during this period (although less and less often) she was in the process of becoming a worldly woman and coming to the final realization that, more than anything, she wanted her independence. In 1918 she left San Francisco forever—heading to Europe to report on post-war conditions there.

Rose Wilder Lane became one of America's leading

writers in the 1920's and 30's. Anything she wrote was eagerly grabbed by her book publishers and by magazines such as *Sunset, Saturday Evening Post, Harper's, Cosmopolitan, Ladies' Home Journal, Good Housekeeping, Country Gentleman,* and *Redbook.* When she wrote for magazines she was invariably featured on the cover.

Probably her most famous book was *Let the Hurricane Roar* (1933). It was on the best seller lists for many years and continuously in print for forty years; today it is back in print under the title *Young Pioneers.* A few of her earlier books were *Henry Ford's Own Story* (1917), *The Making of Herbert Hoover* (1920), and a fictionalized biography of Jack London entitled *He Was a Man* (1925). All of these men were—or became—Rose's personal friends.

During this period she achieved world fame as a writer, travelled extensively and enjoyed a fantastically adventurous life. She became (and remains) a national hero of Albania; she lived there happily for some time and wrote extensively about that primitive country and its indomitable people. Albania's King Zog even asked Rose to become his wife!

In the 1940's, 50's and 60's her fame as a writer continued. After permanently returning to the U.S. she became fascinated with the changing economics of the world and started to examine the roots of social and political ideas. She put aside fiction and began to write of such matters. Her book *The Discovery of Freedom* was enormously influential.

Fighting her own individual fight for equality in a man's world, Rose preceded and anticipated the organized struggle that followed. She did it for herself and by herself but by example destroyed ancient myths. At the age of 79 she was still actively involved, serving as a war correspondent in Vietnam and sending out her reports even while under fire.

When she returned she finally did retire—for three

years—in the south of Texas where the flowers bloom all year around. Restlessness still gnawed at her at the age of nearly 82, however, and she set out on a round-the-world trip in 1968. Just before her ship was to sail from New York she died as she had wished: in her sleep, after a delightful day of visiting with old friends.

****

Also available from
STEIN AND DAY

The Mayflower by Kate Caffrey

Kings and Queens of England by
   Eric R. Delderfield

The Queens of England by Barbara Softly

Joan of Arc: By Herself and Her Witnesses by
   Regine Pernoud

The Volunteer Fire Company, by
   Ernest Earnest

When I Put Out to Sea by
   Nicolette Milnes Walker

****